PAYBACK TIME . . .

''Drop the gun,'' he said, holding him by the arm and throat. ''Drop it!''

Evans struggled against him, desperately trying to twist his pinioned hand and bring the gun to bear on Retnick.

''Tough guy,'' Retnick said, and closed his fingers with all his strength on Evans' wrist.

Evans screamed in pain, the sound of it high and incredulous in his throat, and the gun clattered from his distended fingers to the floor. Retnick hit him in the stomach then, and something brutal and guilty within him savored the impact of the blow and the explosive rush of air from Evans' lungs. . . .

Berkley Books
by William P. McGivern

THE BIG HEAT
THE DARKEST HOUR
ROGUE COP
SHIELD FOR MURDER

THE DARKEST HOUR
William P. McGivern

BERKLEY BOOKS, NEW YORK

This Berkley book contains the complete
text of the original hardcover edition.
It has been completely reset in a typeface
designed for easy reading, and was printed
from new film.

THE DARKEST HOUR

A Berkley Book / published by arrangement with
the author's estate

PRINTING HISTORY
Dodd, Mead edition published 1955
Berkley edition / March 1988

ISBN: 0-425-10695-0

A BERKLEY BOOK ® TM 757,375
Berkley Books are published by The Berkley Publishing Group,
200 Madison Avenue, New York, New York 10016
The name "BERKLEY" and the "B" with logo
are trademarks belonging to Berkley Publishing Corporation.

PRINTED IN THE UNITED STATES OF AMERICA

10 9 8 7 6 5 4 3 2 1

FOR MARIE AND BILL RADEBAUGH
*with whom I have spent many of my
brightest hours*

One

Steve Retnick's release from Sing Sing caused a brief and seemingly casual stir of interest in the file room of the Thirty-First Detective Squad. There were three men present when Sergeant Miles Kleyburg, after a glance at his desk calendar, said: "Today's the day. You think he'll come back here?" There was no particular emphasis in the tone of his voice.

Lieutenant Neville stood in the doorway of his private office packing a short black pipe, and it was difficult to tell from his expression whether or not he had heard Kleyburg's question. He was frowning slightly, and there was an impersonally irritable set to his lean, intelligent features. "You mean Steve," he said at last, and walked past Kleyburg's desk to the wide, dirt-streaked windows that overlooked the river. Lighting his pipe, he stared without enthusiasm at the view. Snow had fallen that morning and a high steady wind had packed it slightly and tightly on the streets and sidewalks. Gulls stood out brightly against the swollen, soot-dark river.

"I don't know about Retnick," Lieutenant Neville said, shaking his head slowly. "He'll want to know about Ragoni. I hope—" Shrugging, he left the sentence incomplete. "He'll do what he wants, I suppose."

"I'll be glad to see him," Kleyburg said, and the lack of inflection in his voice gave the words a curious weight.

1

Neville glanced at him. "I will too," he said, and went about the business of lighting his pipe.

The third man in the room, a detective named Connors, studied a report on his desk and took no part in the conversation. When the lieutenant returned to his office a moment or so later, Connors stretched and got to his feet. He was a tall young man with even features and wavy blond hair. Except for excellent clothes and a certain aloofness in his manner, there was nothing distinctive about his appearance; his face was handsome but blankly so, unrelieved by humor or intelligence.

"I'm going out for a few minutes," he said casually.

Kleyburg, a heavily built man with thin white hair and horn-rimmed glasses, nodded briefly at him but said nothing. He watched Connors saunter through the double doors of the squadroom, with no expression at all on his tired, solid face.

Connors went quickly down the dusty stairs, nodded to the uniformed lieutenant at the desk, and crossed the mean slum street to a small candy store. Edging through a crowd of youngsters at the comics book rack, he walked to the telephone booth at the rear of the shop. He dialed a number and when a voice answered, he said, "Mr. Amato, please. This is Connors." After a short wait another voice spoke to him, and he said, "Connors, Mr. Amato. I just thought I'd remind you. Retnick is out today." Listening then, he smiled faintly at the back of his well-groomed hand. "Sure," he said at last. "I'll find him. I'll take care of it."

Connors replaced the phone and went outside. A cold wind swept down the crosstown block, stirring up flurries of snow. Connors turned his collar up and hurried toward the station.

But Steve Retnick didn't return that day or the next. And along the waterfront and in certain police stations there were men who waited uneasily for him. . . .

It was eight-fifteen the following night when Retnick walked into Tim Moran's saloon on Twelfth Avenue. He stopped just inside the door, a tall, wide-shouldered man who wore cheap clothes and a felt hat pulled down low on his forehead. His face was expressionless as he glanced around, but his eyes were cold and sharp under the brim of his hat.

The place wasn't crowded at that hour; two dockworkers sat at the end of the bar, red-faced men in caps and bulky jackets. Standing between them was a huge, deceptively fat man whose round, childish face was slightly flushed with liquor. He wore an expensive camel's hair coat that accentuated his size, and his voice rumbled over that of the tenor who was singing shrilly of Killarney from the juke box. Retnick knew the big man; he was called Hammy, and before showing up on the waterfront he had made his living as a sparring partner, a punching bag for fighters who had some brains as well as bulk. He was a simple-minded bully, dangerously strong and arrogant. Retnick wasn't interested in him so he turned and walked slowly to the bar.

Tim Moran looked up from a glass he was polishing and his mouth sagged open in surprise. "Steve!" he said, as a smile spread slowly over his small red face. "Steve, boy! Welcome back, boy."

"Thanks, Tim," Retnick said, taking a seat.

"You've not changed at all," Moran said.

This was almost true; the five years in jail hadn't marked him physically. The planes of his dark face were sharp and hard. There was no gray in his close-cut black hair, and his body was like something made of seasoned wood and leather, tough and flexible, designed to endure. But there were changes.

"Five years older," Retnick said, pushing his hat a bit higher on his forehead. Moran looked into his eyes then and saw the change in the man. He said, "Well, let's celebrate, Steve. What'll it be?" He looked away from Retnick as he spoke, troubled by what he had seen in those flat gray eyes. "What'll it be, boy?"

"I'll skip the drink" Retnick said. "I'm looking for Frank Ragoni. Has he been in here?"

"No, Steve, I haven't seen him for a week."

"You know he's missing, I guess."

"Yes, I know that," Moran said. "But it just don't make sense."

"Have you heard any talk about where he might be?"

"Not a word. I'd like to help. I know you were good friends, but—" He shrugged again, watching Retnick's dark, hard face.

"Ragoni finished his shift at midnight," Retnick said. "He was working at Pier Five, in the hold of a North Star Lines ship that night. He never got home. I've talked to his wife. She says he was in a good mood when he left for work. That's all I've found out."

"Why should he up and disappear?" Moran said. "He's got a nice wife and family, and he's the steady type. It don't make sense, does it, Steve?"

"Not yet it doesn't," Retnick said.

The big man in the camel's hair coat rapped on the bar and stared peevishly at Moran. "What do I do for a drink?" he said, his eyes switching to Retnick. "Send you a gold-plated invitation or something?"

Moran smiled quickly. "I was just talking to a friend I haven't seen for a while. What'll it be?"

"Whisky all round," Hammy said, staring at Retnick. "Give your long-lost friend one, too. He looks like he could use it."

"Right away, Hammy."

When the drink was set before him Retnick studied it for a moment or so in silence, realizing that Hammy was still watching him from the end of the bar. The room was silent as Retnick finally lifted the glass, took a sip from it and nodded to Hammy. "Thanks," he said, and the curious little interval of tension dissolved. Hammy began talking to the dockworkers again, and Moran put his elbows on the bar in front of Retnick.

"Watch yourself with him, Steve," he said, rubbing a hand over his mouth to blur the words. "He's mean."

"Who's he working for?"

"Nick Amato."

"I picked up that drink too fast," Retnick said. "Is Amato still riding high?"

"The men in his local stick behind him."

"Do they have any choice?"

Moran found a rag and began to work on the shining surface of the bar. "I sell beer, Steve. To anybody who wants it. I don't take sides in union politics. You know how it is."

"Sure," Retnick said. "I know how it is."

"Steve, this is none of my business, but—" The little Irishman shrugged and smiled uncertainly. "Have you been to see your wife yet?"

Retnick stared at him for a moment or so without any expression on his face. Then he said, "No," in a cold tight voice and got to his feet. "Take it easy," he said, and started for the door.

Hammy called after him, "Hey, you didn't finish your drink, buddy!"

Retnick turned around slowly. "I don't want it," he said.

"That's no way to treat a free drink," Hammy said, studying Retnick expectantly. "Go on, toss it down."

Retnick kept a tight grip on his temper; he couldn't afford trouble with this fool. "You've got a point," he said, and walked to the bar and finished off the drink.

Hammy sauntered toward him then, a little smile touching his big simple face. He was a ponderous bulk of a man, with a chest and stomach that were barrel-like in their proportions. His eyes were small and confident, reflecting the simple trust he held in his own size and strength. He enjoyed the power his huge body gave him over others, and he looked for occasions to exercise it; fighting made him feel brave because he hadn't the wit to distinguish between strength and courage.

"I guess I'm a little slow," he said, still grinning amiably. "You're Steve Retnick, aren't you?"

"That's right," Retnick said turning again toward the door.

"The big tough copper," Hammy said, with a different edge to his voice; he was whetting his temper now, waiting pleasurably for it to take charge of his judgment and senses.

"The big tough cop who got sent to jail for murder. How was it in jail, copper?"

Retnick said, "It wasn't good, Hammy."

Hammy cocked his big head slightly. "You don't sound tough any more," he said. "I guess they softened you up some." There wouldn't be any fight, he knew then. This was a big slob whose guts had turned to water in a cell. "You better get going," he said, leaning against the bar. "I don't like ex-cops any better than I like cops."

Retnick hesitated briefly, memorizing the look of Hammy's big stupid face, the arrogant pose of his body at the bar. "Okay," he said and walked out. The opening and closing of the door let a rush of cold air into the warm bar; a swarm of snowflakes whirled dizzily across the floor before melting into little black spots of water. Hammy put his head back and began to laugh . . .

Outside, Retnick turned his collar up against the bitter wind that came off the river. The graceful bulk of a liner loomed directly ahead of him, blacker than the night. He lit a cigarette, cupping his powerful hands about the match, and the small flame glinted on the sharp planes of his face and drew a vivid outline of his head and shoulders against the darkness. Inhaling deeply he waited for his anger to subside; this was a new anger, hot and impulsive, completely alien to the frozen lifeless anger that had been locked inside him for five years. He could control this new anger, subjugate it to a proper place in his plans. The old anger was something else again; that existed of itself, independent of his will or desire. Flipping the match aside he walked uptown and turned into a slum block, where only a few yellow lights winked from the tall old brownstones.

This was an area he had learned by heart; the river first with its slow booming traffic, and then the piers, the switching yards, the mean tough waterfront streets of the west side. This was a jungle on the edge of the city and Retnick knew most of its secrets.

Retnick walked east for three blocks, occasionally stopping in the shadow of a car to study the street behind him;

but nothing moved in the darkness. In the fourth block he passed the heavy incongruous bulk of St. Viator's and went up the stone steps of the rectory that adjoined the church. For an instant he hesitated before the stained glass cross that was inset in the frosted pane of the door. Then he rang the bell.

Mrs. Simmons, the white-haired housekeeper, opened the door, and when she recognized him she let out a little cry of surprise and pleasure. "Steve, it's really you," she said, as he stepped into the lighted foyer. It was obvious she didn't know quite what to say after that; she made several false starts, stammering with the excitement of it all, and then said, "Wait, I'll tell Father Bristow. Just wait, he's in his study."

Retnick removed his hat and turned down the collar of his overcoat. Brushing flakes of snow from his shoulders, he glanced about the little room, studying the familiar furniture and pictures. Nothing had been changed here. The Madonna, the Crucifix, the faded carpet and old-fashioned hall-tree mirror, they were all the same, just five years older. Everything was five years older.

A door opened and Father Bristow came down the hall, a warm grin spreading on his round brown face. "Well, well, this is wonderful," he said, putting both hands on Retnick's shoulders. "Come on into the study and we'll celebrate properly."

The study was a small room at the back of the rectory, cluttered with books and magazines, smelling of wood smoke and pipe tobacco. Retnick shook his head as Father Bristow took a bottle of wine from a tiny closet beside the fireplace.

"Never mind the drink," he said. "I've got nothing to celebrate."

Glancing at him curiously, Father Bristow saw the cold, dispassionate expression in Retnick's face. He hesitated a second, and then put the bottle away. "All right, Steve," he said quietly.

"I'm looking for Frank Ragoni," Retnick said.

Father Bristow sighed. "I wish I could help you."

"When did you see him last?"

"About two weeks ago."

"Did he have any message for me?"

"No, he and his wife stopped by after Mass, but he didn't have anything specific to say about you, Steve. Their oldest boy is being confirmed pretty soon, and that's what he wanted to see me about."

Retnick was silent a moment, staring at the priest with cold eyes. "Well, it was a long shot," he said. "Thanks, anyway."

"What's all this about?"

"Six weeks ago I had a letter from Ragoni," he said. Staring into the fire, Retnick's eyes narrowed against the small, spurting flames. "He said he knew who killed Joe Ventra."

The silence stretched out between the two men, straining and tight in the cozy little room. Father Bristow was quite pale. "Joe Ventra," he said slowly.

"That's right," Retnick said. "Well, take it easy, father."

"Now wait a minute, Steve," the priest said, putting a hand quickly on Retnick's arm. "What are you going to do?"

"I'm going to find Ragoni. He'll tell me who killed Ventra. After that, everything will be simple."

"Please, Steve. I'm not going to make a sermon, but I want you to listen to me. Everyone knows you didn't kill Joe Ventra. That's common knowledge from one end of the waterfront to the other. You were framed. Everyone knows that."

"That's right," Retnick said, with deceptive gentleness. "I was framed. Everybody knew it. The cops knew it, and so did the unions. But that didn't keep me out of jail. I got thrown off the force as a murderer." Retnick's voice thickened as he jerked his arm away from the priest's hand. "I lived in a cage like an animal for five years," he said, drawing a deep breath. "Sleeping alone, eating what they put in front of me, never moving without rifles pointing at my back. I paid five years of my life for Joe Ventra's death. Now somebody else is going to pay."

"Steve, you're heading for trouble."

"I want trouble," Retnick said, staring at him bitterly. "I need it." And then, because he owed the priest this much, he said, "Forget the guy you remember, father. The guy who taught boxing to your boys clubs and took the kids on fishing trips up to Montauk. I'm somebody else."

"I doubt that," the priest said. "But what about Marcia?"

"She'll get along. She's good at that."

"Aren't you going to see her?"

"Sure," Retnick said. "She knew Ragoni."

"Is that the only reason you're seeing her?"

"Tell me a better one," Retnick said coldly.

A touch of color appeared in the priest's face. "I don't know all your problems," he said, "but I know your duties. And one of them is to treat her with compassion and sympathy, no matter what mistakes she's made."

"And what about her duties?" Retnick said, staring at the priest. Then he turned away sharply. "Talking's no good. I've got to be going, father."

The priest went with him to the door. From the steps he watched Retnick walking toward the avenue, walking like a man advancing on an enemy. Father Bristow shivered involuntarily, not from the cold but from the memory of the coldness in Retnick's eyes.

Two

The Gramercy was a supper club in the east fifties, an intimate spot that featured excellent food and unobtrusive music. There was a small bar and several banquettes at one end of the room to accommodate patrons waiting for tables; it wasn't a place for stags to get drunk in. The bartender looked dubiously at Retnick's cheap suit, and said, "Do you have a reservation, sir?"

"No. Give me a whisky with water."

"Very well, sir." The bartender didn't argue the point; as a judge of men he bet himself that this one wouldn't start any trouble. Finish it, more likely—

Retnick glanced into the crowded, dimly lighted dining room and saw the tiny white piano placed against the far wall.

"When does the music start?" he asked the bartender.

"Nine-thirty, or thereabouts."

"Is she here now?"

"You mean the pianist?"

"That's right, Marcia Kelly."

"I believe she's changing, sir."

Retnick took the paper coaster from under his drink and wrote his name on it. "Would you send this back to her, please?" he said, pushing the coaster across the bar.

"Well, sir, we have a rule about that, you know."

"It's all right. I'm an old friend of hers."

"In this case—" The bartender hesitated, smiling uncertainly. Then he signaled a waiter, hoping that his estimate of the man had been accurate.

The waiter returned in a moment or so and said to Retnick, "She'd like to see you, sir. Will you come with me?"

Walking through the little flurries of laughter and conversation in the dining room, Retnick noticed the piano again and remembered that a piano had figured in their first meeting. This was no feat of memory; there were few details of their days and nights together that he couldn't recall effortlessly and vividly. When he met her he had been birddogging for Father Bristow, looking for someone to give piano lessons to three kids in the boys club. The priest had suggested Marcia Kelly, a girl from the parish who had studied music in college.

She had been willing to help out . . .

They were married in the summer, six months or so after they had met. And a short while after that, a month to the day before Christmas, he was in jail on a murder rap.

They turned into a short corridor and the waiter pointed to a door at the end of it. "Right there," he said.

"Thanks." When the waiter had gone Retnick hesitated, feeling nothing but the pressure of the lifeless anger in his breast. It was all right then, he knew. Nothing could touch him.

He walked down the corridor and rapped on the door. She said, "Come in, please," in a light, expectant voice. Retnick smiled and twisted the knob.

She stood in the middle of the softly lighted dressing room, a small girl with close-cut, curly black hair. There was humor and intelligence in her delicate features, and her body looked slimly mature and elegant in a simple black evening gown.

Retnick closed the door and stood with his back to it, watching her with a cold little smile. For an instant neither of them spoke and the silence became oppressive in the perfume-scented room.

She's twenty-eight now, he thought irrelevantly. The years had touched her; the planes of her face were more sharply defined and the look of gay and careless happiness was gone from her eyes. He noticed that her bare shoulders were lightly tanned but that her face was very pale.

"Steve," she said, and took a tentative step toward him, smiling uncertainly into the coldness of his eyes.

Retnick leaned against the door. "This isn't a social call," he said.

"I waited at home for you yesterday," she said.

"Home?"

A touch of color came into her face. "The apartment then. I—I hoped you'd come back. I had a steak, a bottle of wine—" She made a helpless little gesture with her hands, smiling too brightly now. "It was quite a production, Steve. Too bad you had to miss it."

"A big welcome for the hero, eh?" he said. "The kind GI's get, with all the neighbors in to add to the festivities."

"I thought—"

"I didn't get out of the army, I got out of jail," Retnick said.

She brought her hands up slowly to her breast. "Why didn't you come home?"

"What for?"

"I'm still your wife."

"That's your decision, not mine," Retnick said. "I told you to get a divorce."

"I didn't want a divorce. I wanted to wait for you."

"And did you wait?" Retnick said evenly. "Like a pure and faithful wife in some medieval romance? Is that how you waited?"

"Please, Steve," she said. She turned away from him, hugging her arms tightly against her body. "Let's don't talk about it. Not now. Can't we go somewhere and have a cup of coffee?"

"I don't have time."

"Can't you give me the tiniest break?" she said, turning and looking steadily into his eyes. "I want to tell you what happened. It's not a long and fancy story. There aren't any twists or surprises in it. And I don't come out as the brave and lonely little heroine." She took a step toward him, smiling with trembling lips into his hard face. "I'm not trying to make it sound cute, Steve. You know me better than that."

"I thought I knew you," he said.

"You left me with nothing," she said, shaking her head helplessly. "Why did you do it to me? You told me not to visit you in jail. You wouldn't even see me when I went there. You told me to get a divorce the day the trial ended. And you acted as if you hated me. I couldn't understand it. I tried to wait for you, Steve, I tried. I—"

"There was a man, right?"

"Please, Steve." She turned away from him and put a hand to her forehead. "I wrote you everything. I needed your help. I still need it."

"You needed something," Retnick said, "but it wasn't me. So let's forget it. When did you see Frank Ragoni last?"

She stared at him with something like wonder in her eyes. "What did they do to you, Steve? You used to understand people, you used—"

"When did you see Ragoni last?" Retnick's voice fell across her words like a cold dead weight.

She sat down at the dressing table and shrugged her slim bare shoulders. "Okay, okay," she said wearily. "You think I'm a leper and that's that. I'll stop trying to change your mind. So on to something important. Frank was in here about a month ago, I think. With his wife. They were celebrating an anniversary."

"A month ago. Did he give you any message for me?"

"Nothing in particular."

"Are you sure?"

"I don't know," she said, shaking her head. "What am I supposed to remember?"

"This would have to do with Joe Ventra's murder."

She looked at him and her hand moved slowly to her throat. "I'm sure he said nothing about that."

Retnick hesitated an instant. "Did he ever mention Ventra to you?"

"Only to say you'd been framed for his murder. He said that over and over."

"Did you see Ragoni often?"

"He asked me to come out for dinner every few months. And I had his family up to the apartment occasionally for breakfast after Mass." She smiled bitterly. "We got along fine. He used to tell what a great fullback you were at Fordham. His wife liked me too."

Retnick turned abruptly to the door.

"Steve, wait!" she said, coming swiftly to her feet.

Without looking at her, he said, "I've waited five years. I'm through waiting. So long."

It was ten o'clock when Retnick stepped into a telephone booth a block from the Gramercy. He dialed a number and a woman's voice answered the phone. "I'd like to speak to Mr. Glencannon," Retnick said.

"Who's this?"

"My name is Retnick, Steve Retnick."

"Is there any other message? This is his sister speaking."

"I want to see him tonight, if that's possible."

"Just a moment, please."

Retnick lit a cigarette and waited, staring out at the shining counters of the drugstore, at the couples sitting at the fountain.

"Hello? My brother would be glad to see you tonight. Do you have our address?"

"Yes. I'll be there in about ten minutes."

Retnick left the drugstore and picked up a cruising cab on Lexington Avenue. He gave the driver Glencannon's address and settled back to think. Jack Glencannon was the president of Ragoni's local, 202. And that local was heading for trouble. It adjoined Nick Amato's area of operations, and Amato was preparing to expand in an obvious direction. Retnick had learned this the day before from Frank Ragoni's wife. Amato and Glencannon were as dissimilar as two men could be; one was honest, the other was a thief. But Retnick wondered if Amato were big enough to take on Glencannon; if so it was a tribute of sorts to his nerve and cunning. Glencannon was a tough and powerful old man, a legend

on the docks for more than thirty years. He was Union Jack
to his boys, and they had always stuck to him with fierce
loyalty. Glencannon's hold on his men was simple; he ran
an honest local. He didn't believe in short-gangs, loan
sharks, kickbacks or organized theft. It was a formidable
set-up to oppose, Retnick knew; but he also knew that Amato
never started a fight if there was a chance of losing it.

Glencannon lived on the fifth floor of an apartment building in the west Seventies. Retnick knocked and the door
was opened by a gray-haired woman who smiled and said,
"Come in, please. I'm Jack's sister."

"I'm sorry to be calling so late," he said.

"Goodness, don't let that bother you," she said, with a
little laugh. "People keep coming in at all hours. Friends,
judges, politicians, the mayor himself sometimes, they drop
in when it suits them." She took off her rimless glasses and
smiled philosophically. "I've looked after Jack since my husband died eighteen years ago, and I tell you frankly I marvel
to this day at his patience. Well, now, was it something in
particular you wanted to talk to him about?"

"It's about Frank Ragoni."

"I'll tell him you're here. Please sit down and make yourself comfortable." Then she hesitated. "Jack hasn't been
well lately. I know you'll understand."

Retnick sensed something behind the literal meaning of
her words. "I'll make my visit brief," he said.

Retnick lit another cigarette and glanced about the large,
comfortably furnished room. He had known Glencannon
pretty well in the past. The old man had followed his football
career with interest, and had been one of his references for
the police department. Which certainly hadn't hurt.

The door opened and Glencannon's sister came in. Retnick knew from her expression that something was wrong.

"I'm sorry," she said, making an awkward little gesture
with her hands. "My brother doesn't think he's up to seeing
anyone tonight."

"That's too bad," Retnick said slowly. "Is it anything
serious?"

"No, thank heaven, it's just one of those heavy colds that

is working down to his chest."

"He was all right when I called," Retnick said. "That was ten minutes ago."

"Ups and downs are fairly common at his age," she said, in a cooler voice. "Some other night would be better, I think."

"He didn't go down until he heard Ragoni's name," Retnick said. "Was that what bothered him?"

"It isn't my place to interpret his messages," she said. "He doesn't want to see anyone tonight. That's all I can tell you."

"Maybe the name Ragoni bothers you," Retnick said.

"It means nothing to me."

"You'll be an impartial audience then," Retnick said quietly. "Frank Ragoni was a member of your brother's local. He's been missing for more than a week. Could you guess why?"

"I don't know anything about these matters."

"No, I suppose you don't," Retnick said. "That's why I wanted to talk to your brother. Ragoni is missing, and he may be dead. Maybe he got killed for standing up to Nick Amato. That's not his job, of course, that's your brother's."

"You know all about killing, don't you?" she said, in a rising voice.

"What do you mean?"

"You're Steve Retnick, aren't you?"

Retnick stared at her. "That's right."

She took a step backward, flushing at the look in his eyes. "I didn't mean that," she said. "But you have no right to be badgering me this way. My brother is a sick, over-worked man."

"Tell him I'm sorry for him," Retnick said. "Nick Amato won't be. Goodnight."

Retnick's room was on the first floor of a brownstone that had somehow preserved a remnant of dignity over the years. The wide, high-ceilinged hallway was clean and freshly painted and the beautiful old woodwork had been treated with care; it shone like satin in the light from the ornate brass chandelier. Kleyburg had rented this place in his name a month ago, after checking the landlady's reputation, and making sure that none of the other tenants had police records; this was a parole board requirement and Kleyburg had satisfied it with scrupulous care.

Retnick was searching for his key when a faint scratching noise sounded behind him. He turned quickly, his instincts alerting him to danger, but it was a thin, gray-and-white cat that stared up at him from the shadowed corner of the hallway. It's eyes gleamed like blue-green marbles in the darkness. Retnick let out his breath slowly, and rubbed the back of his hand over his forehead. Relief eased the tension in his arms and shoulders. He knew he was in a dangerous mood, ready to explode at the slightest pressure. But there was nothing he could do about it. He picked up the cat and felt its claws tighten nervously against the rough cloth of his overcoat.

As bad as I am, he thought, rubbing the little animal gently under the chin. But you'll get over it. A cup of milk and a sweater to curl up on will fix you up fine. Shifting the cat to his left hand he opened the door of his room and snapped on the lights. He had nothing to feed her, he realized, and the delicatessens in the neighborhood were closed by now. Annoyed with himself, he turned back to the hallway. He didn't want to be responsible for anything, even a kitten. But he couldn't leave her now. After this promise of attention and company she'd keep the whole house awake scratching and crying at his door. Finally he walked down the hall and rapped gently on his landlady's door. This was a fine way of getting thrown out of here, he thought, waking Mrs. Cara in the middle of the night over a stray cat. But he was wrong. Mrs. Cara opened the door, tightening the belt of her blue robe, and her fat brown face broke into a smile as she saw the cat in Retnick's arm.

"Well, you found Silvy," she said, in a fond pleased voice.

"She was in the hallway. I thought she was probably hungry."

"No, she's been fed. The trouble is she just likes to wander around." She looked up at him then, an appraising little smile on her lips. "Look, you like cats?"

"Well enough," Retnick said. "Why?"

"You could help me out maybe," Mrs. Cara said. "Silvy slips out of here whenever the door is open, and that's practically all the time with the mail, the laundry, and people asking for messages or paying their rent. Then she roams all over the house keeping people awake."

"Well, how can I help out?" Retnick said, as Mrs. Cara paused expectantly.

"Let me keep her in your room. Okay? She won't be no bother, no mess or nothing. I'll take care of her but she lives with you." Smiling, she patted his arm. "How about it?"

Retnick shrugged and smiled faintly. "You made a deal, Mrs. Cara."

"You're a good man," Mrs. Cara said. "Lots of people don't care about cats. They think cats got some trick so they can live without food or any attention at all. 'Drive out in the country and throw 'em anywhere. They'll get by.' That's what some people say. I'd like to throw *them* out in the woods and see how they like it. 'Eat some bark,' I'd tell 'em. 'You'll get along fine.' "

Retnick patted the cat. "We'll see that she gets along okay. Don't worry."

When he returned to his room the cat leaped from his arms and made a tense trip along the walls, peering around as if she expected to find mastiffs in every corner.

Retnick watched her for a few seconds, and then took off his overcoat and dropped it on the bed. By the time he had stripped to the waist the cat was curled up on the coat, blinking drowsily. Smiling faintly he moved her aside and hung his overcoat in the closet. He stretched tiredly then, and the action brought a web of heavy muscles into play; he was built like a weight-lifter, with tremendous arms and shoulders, but there was nothing freakish or narcissistic about the development of his body. He was designed for function, not display.

He was tired but sleep was impossible, he knew; he would only lie staring into the darkness, thinking. And he had done enough of that in the last five years.

He was lighting a cigarette when a knock sounded on the door. Retnick hesitated, frowning. No one had this address but the Parole Board. The knock sounded again, imperatively this time. Retnick stepped to the door and opened it an inch.

"Retnick?" a voice said.

"That's right."

"I'm Connors, Thirty-First Detectives." An open wallet appeared at the crack in the door and Retnick saw the gleaming face of a police shield. "I want to talk to you."

"Sure, come in," he said, opening the door.

Connors studied Retnick, taking his time about it, and then he smiled slightly and sauntered into the room. "Cozy little spot," he said, glancing around casually. "Mind if I take off my coat?"

"Go ahead."

Connors removed his handsomely cut tweed overcoat and folded it neatly over the foot of the bed. When he saw the cat he looked at Retnick with a quizzical little smile. "I didn't figure you as a benefactor of stray kittens," he said.

"How did you figure me?" Retnick said.

Connors shrugged lightly. "You had quite a reputation at the Thirty-First," he said. "Very rugged, very tough." There was just a trace of malice in his smile. "I believe I've heard Sergeant Kleyburg refer to you as quote, a cop's cop, un-quote."

"How is Kleyburg?" Retnick said, ignoring Connors' sarcasm.

"Fine, just fine," Connors said. He sat down and crossed his legs carefully, shifting his trousers to protect their sharp crease. Then he ran a hand over his wavy blond hair and smiled at Retnick. "Is there a drink in the house?"

"Sorry." Retnick found Connors' manner annoying, but he didn't let that show in his expression. He knew nothing about him, but the quality of his clothes was suspicious; the handsome gray flannel suit, the white-on-white shirt, the expensive neatly figured tie—you didn't buy items like that on a detective's salary.

"What are your plans?" Connors said, after lighting a cigarette with a mannered little flourish.

"Nothing definite yet," Retnick said. "Why?"

"I thought I might help you get your bearings," Connors said.

"That would be nice."

Connors was looking for an ashtray. Retnick picked up one from the bureau and Connors accepted it with a nod of thanks. Balancing it on one knee, he looked at Retnick, a small smile touching his smooth handsome face. "Think of this as a briefing," he said. "Things have changed since you went to jail. Specifically, things have changed on the water-front. It will save you time and possibly trouble to keep that in mind. Things are peaceful now. The unions and shippers are getting along, and the locals aren't squabbling among themselves any more. There's a rumble every now and then, but strictly on an intramural basis."

"Intramural?"

"That means all in the family."

"It didn't when I went to college," Retnick said. "But go on."

Connors inclined his head and smiled slightly. "I forgot you weren't an ordinary cop. You were a cop's cop. But as I was saying: the docks are quiet. The man who starts trouble won't have any friends. Do you understand?"

"I think so," Retnick said.

"Good. Another point. Do you have any plans for a job?"

"No."

"Maybe I can help out there." Connors took a deep drag on his cigarette and blew a thin stream of smoke toward Retnick. "When you killed Joe Ventra you inadvertently did Nick Amato a favor. That probably hasn't occurred to you, but Amato is grateful, even though your efforts in his behalf were completely accidental."

"You're sure I killed Ventra," Retnick said.

"I couldn't care less one way or the other," Connors said, with an easy smile. "If you say you took a bum rap, I'll buy that. But the fact is you hit Ventra in a bar, and he went outside and died."

"I pushed him away from me," Retnick said. "He went outside and got slugged to death with a blackjack."

"I'll buy all that," Connors said, still smiling. "As I say, if that's your story it's okay with me. But the jury heard witnesses say you knocked him around brutally, and that he was half-dead when you kicked him into the street. And they found you guilty of murder in the second degree. But to come back to the point: Ventra and Amato were fighting for control of Local 200 at the time. With Ventra dead, Amato naturally took over. *Whoever* killed Ventra accidentally did Amato a favor."

"Maybe Amato did himself a favor," Retnick said.

Connors looked thoughtfully at him. "You're forgetting what I told you already. No one wants trouble. But cracks like that can lead to trouble. For you, my friend."

"Let's get to the point," Retnick said. "What's your deal?"

"Amato's got a job for you. Chauffeur, bodyguard, something like that. The dough is good."

"You like it, I guess," Retnick said

A slow tide of color moved up in Connors' cheeks. "Brother, you are stupid," he said gently. "You're an ex-cop, an ex-convict. You're all washed up. If you start any trouble you'll get your head knocked right off your shoulders."

Retnick turned away slowly, grinding a big fist into the palm of his hand. "You punks all sound alike," he said, in a low, savage voice. "Messenger boys, carrier pigeons, doing dirty little jobs for hoodlums so you can dress like dudes and sneak a few week ends off in Miami or Atlantic City. Who's going—"

"Listen—"

"Shut up!" Retnick said, turning swiftly and dangerously. The anger was a tight cruel pain inside him, a pressure screaming for release. "Who's going to knock my head off? You?"

Connors got to his feet, wetting his lips. Instinct warned
him his gun and badge wouldn't prevail here. "Don't fly
off the handle," he said, smiling with an effort into the
murder in Retnick's face. "I've told you what Amato is
thinking. What you do about it is up to you."

"You can tell Amato I've got a job," Retnick said. "I'm
going to find Frank Ragoni, and I'm going to find out who
killed Ventra. And the guy who killed Ventra is going to
wish to God he'd shot himself the same night."

Connors shrugged and picked up his overcoat. "I gave
you good advice," he said. "You'll probably appreciate it
eventually." Then, in the doorway, he smiled at Retnick.
There was a new confidence in his manner. "Part of that
job you mentioned won't be too difficult. Finding Ragoni,
I mean."

"What's that?"

"You'll see it in the papers. Ragoni's body was pulled
out of the river tonight. I saw the report on it before I came
over here. Someone stuck a knife into him." Connors sighed.
"Those things happen, Retnick. Good night." He closed the
door.

Retnick sat down slowly on the edge of the bed and rubbed
his forehead with the back of his hand. Ragoni was dead.
Connors wouldn't lie about it. For an instant he felt a curious
surprise at his own lack of reaction. Ragoni had been a good
friend of his, but he felt no sense of pain or loss at all,
nothing but a certain selfish disappointment; this would make
his job far more difficult. He swore bitterly and pounded a
fist into his palm. It would have been so easy. Find Ragoni,
listen to a name. That was all. Now he was on his own.
There would be no help for him on the waterfront, no friends.
The cat had curled up beside him but he was unaware of
its warm presence. He sat perfectly still, staring at his big
hands, and the single bare bulb drew deep shadows under
his bitter, lonely eyes.

Three

At midnight Nick Amato sat behind his desk, slumped deep in the chair, with one foot propped up against a pulled-out drawer. The strong overhead light filled the small office with harsh brilliance, revealing cracks in the uncarpeted floor, the worn spots on the furniture, and the chipped gilt lettering on the windows that read: Headquarters, Local 200.

Joe Lyre stood with his back to the wall, his hands deep in the pockets of his black overcoat, and watched the single door.

Amato was studying a Christmas card, a small frown on his broad, swarthy face. Smiling at him from the card was a photograph of his own face, looking absurd under a Santa Claus hat. The inscription read: Happy Holiday Greetings From Uncle Nick.

"This stinks," Amato said, glancing at Joe Lye. "It's cheap. Why did you use my picture? I'm not running for office."

"Okay, I'll tell Dave to take it back to the printer," Joe Lye said.

"The picture would be in every ash can in the neighborhood after Christmas. Great, eh? Figure out something else."

"Okay," Joe Lye said.

Amato tossed the Christmas card on his desk and glanced at his watch. Then he yawned comfortably, a stockily built man of fifty, slightly below middle height, with a face as

23

dark and hard as mahogany. Except for his eyes, which were cynical and pitiless, he could have passed for any sort of small businessman. He usually wore cheap brown or gray suits, and his only curious mannerism was an occasional air of abstraction; he gave the impression that he was listening with amusement to some invisible storyteller.

"How old is Glencannon?" he said, glancing again at Joe Lye.

"I don't know. Seventy-five maybe."

Amato shook his fingers gently in front of his face. "That's too old to be up this time of night," he said.

"Did it have to be tonight?"

"Yeah, tonight, tonight, right away," Amato said, and yawned again. Then he began to laugh.

"What's funny?" Joe Lye asked him, not sure of what to expect. You never knew with Amato when he was in these dreamy moods. Sometimes he wanted to talk, sometimes he wanted you to shut up. You never knew.

"Glencannon is worried," Amato said, smiling gently. "He can't wait till morning. Maybe he wants to give us 202."

"*I* wish he'd waited till morning," Lye said. He crossed the room, a thin figure in black, and leaned against the wall. His eyes were irritable in the unhealthy pallor of his small, lean face. There was the suggestion of a smile about his lips but this was a matter he couldn't control; a tic pulled his mouth into a tight grimace when he was nervous or worried. It looked like a grin at first glance, but the illusion of humor was shattered by the dangerous tension in his face.

"*You* wish he'd waited till morning?" Amato said. "What was you doing that was so important?"

"Well, I don't go to Kay's to watch television," Lye said. He wished he'd kept his mouth shut; Amato loved this little game.

"What was you doing?" Amato said.

"Getting ready to eat, if you want details."

"This late?"

"Sure." Lye gestured nervously with a slim pale hand. "I didn't get there till nine. We had a few drinks, Martinis, if you're interested, and she was just ready to put in the steak when you called."

"Martinis and steaks," Amato said, smiling and shaking his head slowly. "Just like the movies. You got the life, Joe. Not like it was in jail, eh?"

Lye felt his mouth twisting painfully. Lighting a cigarette he changed his position against the wall, turning the unmarked side of his face to Amato; it filled him with a sick rage to be stared at. "Why talk about jail?" he said, flipping the burned match across the room.

"Because it's getting interesting," Amato said, watching Lye with a little grin. "Those guards up there used to tell me how you were doing."

"I know, I know," Lye said. "They should keep their big fat mouths shut."

"They said you prayed every night," Amato said. "Down on your knees like you was in a church. That's funny, eh?"

"You got a funny idea of what's funny."

"What were you praying for?"

"The place gets you," Lye said. He looked quickly around the room, his eyes switching like those of an animal in a trap. Since those two weeks in the death cell a dream the color of blood had plagued his sleep, turning every night into an occasion of potential terror. It was always in red, a dull crimson shot with flecks of black, and there were laughing guards who rushed him down the corridor to the chair. Only it wasn't a chair when they reached it, but a high rude altar, and they stretched him on it and tightened the straps about his body until his couldn't breathe.

"It must be pretty bad," Amato said, shaking his head. "But I don't get the praying business. What's that going to help?"

"I don't know," Lye said, dropping his cigarette on the floor. "The place softens you up, that's all. You act buggy."

Amato said casually, "You ought to get your face fixed up, Joe. It looks like hell, you know."

"Sure I know," Lye said, rubbing his mouth nervously. "You think I like it? But the doc says it's in my head."

"He thinks you're nuts?"

"He's the nutty one if you ask me," Lye said. Relax, the doctor said. But how could he relax when he couldn't even sleep?

"You shouldn't have worried in jail," Amato said. "Didn't you know I'd get you out?"

"Time was getting short," Lye said.

"Trust me," Amato said. "Don't waste time praying to anybody else. Well, what about Retnick?"

"Connors talked to him," Lye said. He felt the tension easing in his straining lips. "Retnick's in no mood to play ball. Connors couldn't get anything definite from him."

"That Connors never has anything definite," Amato said. "It's getting bad when you can't buy anything better than a dummy like Connors."

"Retnick's got a one-track mind. He's still thinking about who killed Ventra."

Amato frowned slightly at the top of his desk. "That's a Polack for you," he said. "Stubborn."

A step sounded on the stairs and Amato raised a hand quickly for silence. But it was Hammy who opened the door and sauntered into the room, a drunken grin on his big red face. "Sorry I'm late," he said to Amato, and slumped into a chair that creaked under his great weight.

"Where've you been?" Amato said, in a deceptively pleasant voice.

"Around. Here and there." Hammy laughed and massaged his bumpy forehead with the back of his hand. "Celebrating."

"I didn't say twelve o'clock just to be talking."

The look in Amato's eyes sobered Hammy. "Sure thing, boss, it won't happen again. I—"

"Okay, *okay*," Amato said, cutting him off irritably. "Joe, you figure something for Retnick."

"All right," Lye said.

Hammy was smiling. "Retnick? That guy couldn't lick his upper lip. I can take him, boss."

"Where? To a movie, maybe?"

"I deliver, you know that." Amato's sarcasm didn't diminish Hammy's childish confidence in his own ability.

There were many things his small brain didn't understand; but he understood perfectly well that he could kill most men in a matter of seconds with his hands. Not in a ring maybe, but an alley or barroom was different.

A bell jangled from below, and Amato said, "Well, here's the old man. Go bring him up, Hammy."

"Sure, Boss."

Amato smiled faintly at Lye as they heard the slow, heavy footsteps ascending the stairs. "We should have had an oxygen tent handy," he muttered.

The door opened and Jack Glencannon came into the room, blinking at the harsh overhead light.

"Take a seat," Amato said, staring at the old man's flushed face. "You don't look so chipper."

"The stairs get my wind these days," Glencannon said, taking a deep breath. He sat down slowly and patted his damp forehead with a handkerchief.

"Relax a second," Amato said, smiling coldly. "You're no spring chicken any more. You should be soaking up the sun in Florida on a nice pension. Maybe it's time to let somebody else run your local."

The old man straightened his shoulders then and tried to put a suggestion of defiance into the thrust of his big jaw. But it was a futile effort. Everything about Glencannon was old and weary and beaten; the clothes hung loosely on his once-powerful frame, and there was a good inch of space between his collar and the withered skin of his throat. Networks of tiny blue veins had ruptured in his cheeks; he had been drinking heavily that night, and for many nights in the past, but he hadn't numbed himself sufficiently for this showdown. There was a core of fear in him that the liquor hadn't been able to dissolve.

"We need a frank talk, Amato," he said, trying for a hearty tone. "We've needed it for a long time." He hesitated then, conscious of Lye's bright stare, and Amato's supercilious smile. "I guess you know what I mean," he said.

"You're talking," Amato said. "Keep going."

"We don't have to fight each other," Glencannon said, smiling with obvious effort. "Some of your boys are pressur-

ing the men in my local—I guess we both know that, Nick.
And it's got to stop.''

Amato didn't answer him for a moment. Then he said
gently, ''*You* say it's got to stop. Okay. *You* stop it, then.''

''It's your men that need the stopping,'' Glencannon said,
standing and putting his hands on Amato's desk for support.
''I don't hire the likes of your bums and hoodlums. You tell
'em to keep away from my local. It's a clean place. The
men are satisfied. They don't want killers with guns telling
'em how to vote.''

''Killers?'' Amato said, raising his eyebrows. ''That's a
pretty strong word, old man.''

Glencannon stared at Amato, his breathing loud and harsh
in the silence. ''Frank Ragoni didn't stab himself in the back
and jump into the river,'' he said.

''You're talking real stupid,'' Joe Lye said.

''Shut up,'' Amato said casually. ''You think we killed
Ragoni?''

''He was told to get off the docks by your men,'' Glencannon said, struggling to keep his voice steady. ''He was told
to stop talking about the elections. He got a last warning.
Shut up or get killed. He didn't shut up, and he got a knife
in his back.''

Amato leaned forward, and his face settled into cold ugly
lines. ''Now listen to me, you washed up old slob,'' he said,
softly and quietly. ''You want your local, you fight for it.
Elections are next month. The boys will make their choice.
That's all there is to it. I got nothing else to say to you.''

''Wait a minute, Nick. I didn't come here to start a fight.
This thing can be worked out peacefully.'' Glencannon's
smile was a travesty; his lips were pulled back against his
teeth but his eyes were bright with fear. ''We're on the same
side, after all. We're union men, Nick. How will it look
for us to be squabbling? I—''

''I told you I had nothing more to say.'' Amato stood up
and stared with distaste at the old man's trembling lips.
''You're a drunk and a slob and I'm tired of looking at you.
Now beat it.''

Glencannon fought to say something, anything, but there

were no more words in his sick, tired old mind. Thirty years ago, he thought, remembering what he had once been, seeing again the man who could shout down a hall full of workers, and if necessary enforce his orders with rock-hard fists. He put a hand to his forehead and took an involuntary step backward, wanting nothing now but to get away from the contempt and anger in Amato's eyes. "You didn't understand me, Nick," he said weakly.

"Take him home, Hammy," Amato said.

"No. I'll look after myself."

"You need a nurse. Take him home, Hammy."

When they had gone Amato shook his head and sat down at his desk. "He'd do himself a favor if he laid down and died," he said.

"You handled him right," Joe Lye said.

"Hell, a two-year-old baby could handle him," Amato said. "But he used to be quite a boy. Years ago, that was. Well, turn out the lights. You can drive me home."

"Look, Kay is waiting for me," Lye said, and wet his lips. "I mean, she's right downstairs."

Amato was getting into his heavy black overcoat. He stopped, one arm in a sleeve, and looked blankly at Lye. "How come she's here?" he said at last.

"She drove me down and I told her to wait," Lye said. Anger ate at him like a corrosive acid. Amato was playing the puzzled peasant now, one of his most maddening roles. Everything would have to be spelled out for him in capitals. "You said to hurry," he explained. "I thought I'd make better time if she drove me."

"And she waited for you?"

"Well, I didn't think we'd be long."

"I see." Amato nodded and finished putting on his coat. "You don't want to drive me, is that it?"

"No. I'll tell her to go on home."

"It's no trouble?" Amato was smiling slightly.

"Of course not."

"Where does she live?"

"On the east side. Near Park." He knew damn well where she lived, Lye thought bitterly.

"Pretty fancy neighborhood," Amato said shaking his head. "You're flying high, Joe."

"Well, it's her place, not mine."

Amato smiled cynically. "What does she pay the bills with? She ain't been in a show in ten years. How old is she anyway?"

Lye felt his mouth tightening. Turning away from Amato he said, "She's thirty-five."

Amato laughed and strolled to the door. "Yeah," he said. "Well, let's go."

Lye went downstairs ahead of him, his footsteps clattering noisily through the silent building, and Amato smiled as he snapped off the lights. The smile lingered on his lips as he went slowly down to the first floor.

Moving with short jerky strides, Lye crossed the street to the gray convertible that was parked in the darkness opposite union headquarters. He rapped his knuckles against the window and the girl at the wheel rolled the glass down quickly.

"What is it, Joe?" she said. "What's the matter?"

"Nothing the matter," he said in a low tense voice. "Does there have to be something the matter? You always act like the world's about to blow up in your face."

"Joe," she said pleadingly.

"I got to drive him home," he said. "I'll be up later."

"Sure, Joe." She was a pretty blonde woman, expensively cared for, but her eyes were miserable with fear. "Don't get excited," she said, and touched his hand gently. "Is he riding you again?"

"I got to take him home, that's all," he said, spacing the words deliberately and coldly. "Why do you make a Federal case out of everything?"

"I know what he does to you," she said.

"Will you stop it?"

"All right, Joe. But hurry."

"I'll make it as soon as I can."

Amato stood in the darkness across the street, listening to the murmur of their conversation. He saw the small pale blur of her face, and the pearls gleaming at her throat. Kay

Johnson, he thought, turning the name slowly in his mind. He had seen her in a movie once, back in the late Thirties.

She wasn't a very good actress, but she was damn good-looking, one of those long-legged, pink-and-white college-kid types, full of healthy sex and bounce. Amato had met her a couple of times with Joe, but always briefly. She was thin and elegant now, with a shining blonde hair-do, and very classy clothes. Nice for Joe, he thought. Too nice for Joe.

The engine turned over, filling the dark silence with the sound of power, and Joe Lye crossed the street and joined Amato on the sidewalk. When the car was halfway down the block, Amato said abruptly, "I'll take myself home."

Lye turned and stared after the red tail lights of her car.

"You can't catch her," Amato said irritably. "Get a cab."

"Sure," Lye said. He was breathing hard, but his anger was dissolving in relief and anticipation. "You sure you're okay?"

"For Christ's sake, yes."

"I'll see you in the morning."

Amato put his hands in his pockets and watched Lye hurrying off into the darkness, his thin black figure moving in a jerky, puppet's rhythm. In a sour and bitter mood, Amato finally turned and walked down the block to his sedan. With a conscious effort he tried not to think of the home he was going to, the cluttered, close-smelling apartment with its profusion of holy pictures and expensive, tasteless furniture. He shook his head quickly, as if trying toi dislodge a disagreeable memory. Money meant nothing to his wife. If he gave her a hundred dollars she'd buy something for their nephew, or drop it in the poor box. Nothing for herself but a black dress that looked just like every other black dress she'd bought in the last twenty years. Amato slid behind the wheel of his car and made an attempt to change the direction of his thoughts. He didn't want to be envious of Joe Lye. That could mean trouble.

Four

At seven o'clock Retnick left his room and walked to a restaurant on the avenue for breakfast. The day was cold and beautiful; clean winter sunlight sparkled on the snow in the gutters and brightened the faces of the old brownstones. When he returned Mrs. Cara was waiting for him in the hall.

"There's a telephone call for you," she said. "The woman says she's your wife."

Retnick hesitated and Mrs. Cara watched his dark hard face with frank curiosity. "Okay," he said at last.

"And how was the cat?" Mrs. Cara said, catching his arm. "No trouble, eh?"

"No, not a bit."

"See? I told you," she smiled.

Retnick said, "That's right," and walked down the hall to the telephone.

"Hello," he said.

"Steve—I saw the story on Frank," she said quietly. "I'm terribly sorry. I know what you meant to each other."

"Sure," he said. Then: "Where did you get this number?"

"From Lieutenant Neville. Steve, I want to go out to see Mrs. Ragoni this afternoon." She hesitated, then said tentatively, "Would you come with me?"

"I'm going to be busy," he said.

"Please, Steve, I want to talk to you. Last night was so terribly wrong."

"What do you want to talk about?" he said.

"Steve, Steve," she cried softly, and he knew that she was weeping. "Don't throw everything away. Won't you let me see you this morning?"

He hesitated, frowning at the phone. "Okay," he said at last. "I'll stop by Tim Moran's saloon around ten. Can you make that?"

"Yes, yes, of course."

Retnick put the phone down, irritated with himself. He didn't want to see her, not for any reason.

Twenty minutes later Retnick walked into a sturdy, red-brick station house on the west side of the city. Nothing important had been changed, he noticed, as he stopped at the high wooden information desk. A new painting of the flag hung above the switchboard where a sergeant worked in contact with the district's squads and patrolmen. But everything else looked the same.

"Is Lieutenant Neville in?" he asked the lieutenant behind the desk.

"He's upstairs in the Detective division. Take the stairs at the end of the hall."

Sergeant Kleyburg was sitting alone in the long file room, frowning at a bulky report on his desk. When Retnick stopped at the counter that divided the office, Kleyburg glanced up and removed the horn-rimmed glasses from his broad, impassive face. Then he said, "I'll be damned," in a horse, surprised voice. He crossed the room, grinning, and pushed open the gate at the end of the counter. "Come in, boy," he said.

They shook hands and Retnick glanced around at the familiar dusty furniture, the height chart, the bank of gray steel filing cabinets, the bulletin board with its cluster of yellowing flyers.

"It hasn't changed much," he said, looking at Kleyburg.

"You haven't either," Kleyburg said, punching him lightly on the arm. "You look great."

"I feel great," Retnick said.

Kleyburg nodded slowly, his eyes grave and hard. "I can imagine, Steve. You took a lousy rap."

"You should have been on the jury," Retnick said. "Is the lieutenant busy?"

"Hell, no. You want to see him alone?"

"It doesn't matter. But one thing first. Do you have a detective here named Connors?"

"He's on my shift."

"Does he work for anyone else?"

Kleyburg shrugged. "I couldn't prove it. That answer your question?"

"Yeah," Retnick said. "He's real smart, eh?"

Kleyburg shrugged again. "We get smart ones occasionally. You know that. They don't last long. Let's go see the boss."

Lieutenant Neville, a slim man with an air of competence about him, looked up from his desk when they opened the door of the office. "Well, well," he said, standing and grinning at Retnick. "You should have given us a little warning. We could have had drinks and dancing girls. How the devil are you, Steve?"

"Fair enough," Retnick said.

"I suppose you don't have any plans yet," Neville said.

"Oh, yes," Retnick said, staring at him. "I'm going to find out about Ragoni."

A small silence settled in the room. Kleyburg shifted his weight from one foot to the other, and Neville ran a hand slowly over his thinning brown hair. "That was rough," he said. "I know you were friends." He picked up a report from his desk, frowned at it for a second, and then offered it to Retnick. "That's all we have so far," he said.

Retnick skimmed through the detective's report, picking out the important information quickly. Body of deceased had been observed by a barge captain, floating just under the surface of the river at Eighty-seventh Street. Identification had been made by wife of the deceased. Cause of death was listed as knife wounds.

"That's all you've got, eh?" Retnick said, dropping the report on Neville's desk.

"We just found his body last night."

"You haven't questioned Nick Amato, of course," Retnick said gently.

"Why the 'of course'? We'll pick him up if there's a reason to, Steve."

"He's moving in on Glencannon's local," Retnick said. "Ragoni was warned to stop lobbying against Amato and his hoodlums. Now Ragoni's dead. I'd say this is a good time to pick up Nick Amato."

"You don't pick up Nick Amato with a case like that," Neville said. "Now listen to me, Steve. I'm a cop, not a tea-leaf reader. And I've got to talk to you like a cop. You get in trouble with Amato and I won't be able to help you out of it. Do you understand?"

"I'm not asking for help," Retnick said.

Neville's face was troubled. He came around the desk and put a hand on Retnick's arm. "Don't be so touchy," he said. "Off the record, I'll do what I can. And I think that goes for Kleyburg here and lots of other cops. But officially you're an ex-cop and an ex-con. Those are two strikes against you, Steve. Keep that in mind."

Retnick smiled coldly. "There's not much chance of forgetting it. Take it easy, Lieutenant."

"Now don't barge off this way," Neville said, tightening his grip on Retnick's arm. "Calm down and listen to me. Will you do that?"

"I'll listen," Retnick said.

Neville sat on the edge of his desk and took out his pipe. "You're thirty-three now, right?"

"That's right."

"You've got a long life ahead of you. Don't throw it away, Steve."

"A long life," Retnick said. "And what do I do with that nice long life?"

"You can start over, Steve."

"The big bright dream," Retnick said, staring at him with a bitter smile on his lips. "Work hard, make good. I did that once, remember? I worked my way through school, and earned eight major letters while I was doing it. I took the police exams when I was twenty-two, and was a third-grade detective eighteen months later. Working hard, making good. I've had enough of it. Let somebody else work hard and make good. I've got other plans."

Neville was silent a moment, staring at his unlighted pipe. Then he said: "Do those plans include your wife?"

"No," Retnick said. "They concern the guy who killed Joe Ventra."

"Steve, you're heading for trouble."

Retnick started to say something, but changed his mind. He made a short, chopping gesture with his hand, and said, "Why waste each other's time? Take it easy, Lieutenant."

Kleyburg followed him down the stairs and caught up with him on the sidewalk. He blinked into the bright sunlight and said, "Steve, if you need anything, just yell. Remember that. Anything."

Retnick said, "Is Ben McCabe still the super over at the North Star Lines?"

"Yes. Why?"

"That's where Ragoni worked," Retnick said. "It's the last place he was seen alive. It's a good place to ask a question or two."

Kleyburg's eyes were worried. "Watch yourself, boy."

The North Star Lines terminal boomed with noise and commotion; two ships were loading that morning, and winches, trucks and men were straining against the inflexible pressure of time and tides. Retnick stopped before the checker's office and here, at the mouth of the cavernous warehouse, the noise beat against him in waves.

A guard in a leather jacket stepped out of the office and looked at Retnick with close, sharp eyes.

"Is Ben McCabe around?" Retnick said.

"Yeah, but they got two ships working. He's pretty busy. What'd you want to see him about?"

"Tell him Steve Retnick is looking for him."

"Will that be enough?"

"Let's try it," Retnick said.

The guard shrugged and said, "You wait here." He walked

onto the pier and turned out of sight around a wall of cargo. In a minute or so he reappeared and said, "It's okay, Retnick. You know the way?"

"I can find him," Retnick said. The terminal was cold and drafty; above the whine of winches and rumble of trucks the wind sang through the superstructure of the ships, and swept refuse in frantic eddies along the thick planking of the floor. The air smelled of coffee and oil and the river. Retnick turned into an aisle formed by crates of cargo and went up a flight of steps to McCabe's office, which over-looked the length of the pier. McCabe's chief clerk, a thin, balding man with a shy smile said, "Well, Steve, it's nice to see you again."

His name was Sam Enright, Retnick remembered. They shook hands and Enright said, "Go right on in. The boss is expecting you."

"Thanks, Sam."

McCabe stood up when Retnick entered his office, a short, stockily built man in his fifties, with thick, gray hair and a bold, good-humored face. "I didn't expect to see you for a couple of months," he said, as they shook hands. "I thought you'd go off on a long fishing trip or something. You look fine though, like you'd been fishing instead—" He smiled apologetically and didn't finish the sentence.

"Well, I was up the river anyway," Retnick said.

McCabe smiled. "Sit down. What's on your mind?"

"I want to find out about Ragoni."

McCabe said slowly, "You know he's dead, I guess."

"I heard about it last night. That's why I'm here."

McCabe wasn't smiling now; his manner was cautious. "You probably know as much as I do, Steve. Ragoni was last seen in the hold of the *Santa Domingo*, nine days ago around midnight. He went on deck and didn't come back. The crew thought he'd gone home." He hesitated and shrugged. "The next day we learned that he hadn't gone home. Last night we learned that he'd been murdered. It's a police matter from now on."

"How about the accident a couple of weeks ago?" Retnick

said, casually. "Was someone trying to get Ragoni then?"

McCabe's eyes narrowed slightly. "Who told you about an accident?"

"I spent my first afternoon out of jail at Ragoni's home," Retnick said. "His wife told me about the accident."

"Well, there was an accident, as you obviously know," McCabe said. "We investigated it thoroughly. It was a mix-up in orders. The winchman lowered a draft while Ragoni was on the loading platform. Fortunately, he saw it coming and got clear."

"Did you notify the police?"

"That isn't customary, as you know." McCabe's manner was cold and sharp. There were spots of color in his cheeks.

"You know Amato's moving onto your pier, don't you?" Retnick said.

McCabe stood up abruptly and said, "That's a matter I won't discuss."

"Which means the answer is yes," Retnick said.

"Neither yes or no," McCabe said, coming around his desk. We're shippers. We're not philosophers of labor, and we aren't police officers. We work with what the unions give us. I wish the public understood that. Union squabbles aren't our concern."

"Sure," Retnick said coldly. "And because of that Ragoni is dead."

"I don't like the implications," McCabe said angrily.

"I don't like it either," Retnick said. "It stinks, if you ask me. Ragoni was fighting as an individual to keep Amato's killers from taking over the place he worked. They warned him to keep quiet, but he wouldn't. So they tried for him with a few tons of cargo, and then they stuck a knife in his back. And the same will happen to any man who doesn't want to take orders from Amato's stooges."

McCabe turned away and ran a hand through his hair. "All right, all right," he said bitterly. "If Amato wins the election he's in. He supplies our terminal. And what in hell can we do about it?"

"You could close down the pier and ship out of Boston

or Philly," Retnick said. "You could post a notice that you wouldn't come back to the city until Amato's killers were out of the union. How would that sit with your stockholders?"

"You guess," McCabe said.

"Well, I didn't come here to tell you your business," Retnick said. "I need a favor."

"What's that?"

"I want to talk to Ragoni's crew."

"Why?"

Retnick shrugged. "I was a good friend of his."

McCabe hesitated, staring with worried eyes at the river that flowed sluggishly past his windows. "Put it that way, and it's all right. But this can't be official, Steve. You understand my position, I think."

"Sure. Can I see them now?"

"Come with me. Ragoni's crew is on the *Executive*."

Retnick followd McCabe downstairs to the pier. Ahead of them the terminal jutted out a hundred yards into the river, a peninsula of noise and light and movement. The *Executive* was loading to their right, its long graceful hull curving high above the docks.

Retnick and McCabe walked down an aisle flanked by small mountains of cargo, and boarded her amidships. The wind hit them with buffeting force as they stepped from a companionway to the ship's unsheltered aft deck. At the moment cargo was being stacked in the hold, and the winchman and deck gang were idle; they stood about the open hatch with their hands in their pockets and shoulders hunched against the weather. A big man in a leather windbreaker walked over to them and tugged the brim of his cap.

"Everything's on schedule, Mr. McCabe," he said.

"Fine. Brophy, this is Steve Retnick."

Brophy tilted his big square head to one side and studied Retnick with narrow eyes. "I think we met," he said. "Didn't you used to be at the Thirty-First?"

"That's right."

"What can I do for you?" Brophy said. Several men

drifted over and fanned out in a semicircle behind him, their eyes flicking curiously from Brophy to Retnick.

"I was a good friend of Frank Ragoni and his family," Retnick said. "His wife is in pretty bad shape right now, as you can imagine."

"Sure." Brophy nodded, and several of the men behind him murmured appropriately.

"I talked to her this morning," Retnick said. "The only thing on her mind was an accident Frank had had on the job a few weeks ago. The doctor told me that this kind of thing is common in shock cases. She was trying to think about anything except the fact that Frank was dead. To calm her down, I told her I'd come over and talk to Mr. McCabe about it. He was good enough to let me see you boys."

His words made an impression on the men. They all looked solemn and thoughtful. Brophy said, "I can tell you about the accident, Retnick. But it wasn't an accident, I guess you know. It was a near-miss. I was in the hold next to Ragoni when it happened. There was some dunnage on the loading platform and Ragoni said something about it. I guess he asked if he should pick it up. Well, I'd already given the signal to lower away, so I said never mind." Brophy took a deep breath that filled his body out like a circus fat man's. "But he didn't hear me, I guess. Or he misunderstood. He scrambled onto the platform just as the winch let the draft go. It missed Ragoni by an inch or two. That's the story, Retnick, all of it."

Retnick nodded. "I know how those things happen. By the way, who was on the winch?"

"An extra man, fellow name of Evans. Grady here had been out sick for a week or so."

"I had the flu," a red-faced little man in the group said importantly. "Couldn't get out of bed for two weeks."

Retnick looked at him. "Did you know this fellow Evans?"

The question seemed to put Grady on the defensive. He looked from side to side as if expecting an attack from either direction. "No, I didn't know him. He was a new man."

"Did you know him, Brophy?"

"Me?" Brophy looked surprised. "No. Steinkamp, our hiring boss, picked him out of the shape when Grady called in sick. Evans knew his stuff, that's all I cared about."

Retnick didn't ask any more questions. He sensed that the mention of Evans had changed the mood of the men.

"Thanks a lot," he said to Brophy. "I won't take up any more of your time."

They walked back to the terminal office through the noise that crashed between the iron hulls of the two big liners. McCabe sat on the edge of his desk and looked at Retnick.

"That's as much as I can do for you," he said. "You heard the story. It's straight."

"Yes, I think it is," Retnick said. He shrugged and smiled. "Thanks a lot, Mac."

"Anytime, Steve."

Retnick nodded good-by to him and left his office. Sam Enright glanced up from his desk in the outer room and said, "Well, the boss looks pretty good, wouldn't you say?"

"Yes, he does," Retnick said.

"I suppose it's too early to ask about your plans."

"I'm going to loaf for a while." Retnick sat on the edge of Enright's desk and lit a cigarette. "By the way, what kind of fellow was Evans?"

Enright ran both hands over his bald head, and then frowned as if he were both surprised and a little hurt to find that his hair was gone. "Well, Evans wasn't here more than eight or ten days. He was a big guy, a redhead. They called him Red. Quite a hot-tempered character, I heard. Why?"

"I think I knew a friend of his in jail. Do you have an address for Evans?"

"Just a minute." Enright went to a filing cabinet and took out a card. "We have the dope on him because of the accident. Normally these extra men just float in and out. Got a pencil? He had a room on Tenth Avenue. 201, Tenth. Got it?"

"Yes, thanks. When did he leave here?"

"About a week ago, I think."

Right after Ragoni disappeared, Retnick thought. "Well,

it may not be the same guy," he said casually.

"From what I heard of Red Evans you're lucky if it isn't," Enright said.

Retnick smiled, but his eyes were cold and deadly. "We'll see," he said.

Outside Retnick crossed the avenue and waited for a cab. Traffic was heavy now; trucks rattled by him in steady streams, rushing the city's supplies to terminals, docks, freight yards. The sun had gone under a bank of low black clouds, and the day was stark and cold. Retnick's hunter's senses told him he had struck a hot trail; it was hardly coincidence that Evans and Ragoni had disappeared at the same time. This was a lead the police might not come across. There was no report of the near accident and the longshoremen, even Ragoni's friends, wouldn't be likely to mention it. The penalties for talking were too high.

Evans' attempt to kill Ragoni a week before would be smothered in silence. And the facts would change mysteriously; the file on him might disappear from Enright's office, and men would remember him as dark-haired and small, if they remembered him at all.

Retnick flagged a cab and gave the driver Evans' Tenth Avenue address. It was a run-down rooming house crowded in between a small factory and a dead storage garage for automobiles. He talked with Evans' erstwhile landlady, a plump middle-aged woman with an orderly enthusiasm for detail. Evans had been with her for a month to the day, and had checked out a week ago. He was a man who kept mostly to himself; she only saw him when he stopped by to pay his weekly rent. But he kept his room neat, which wasn't surprising since he seldom slept there. She didn't know where he slept.

"Is he in some kind of trouble?" she asked him at last.

Retnick smiled. "Just the opposite. We've got some money for him on a damage claim he filed last year."

"Oh. Well, I wish I could help you."

"Did he send his laundry out in the neighborhood?"

"Yes, I believe he took it around to the Chinaman's.

That's in the middle of the next block."

"Thanks a lot," Retnick said. "If I catch up with him I'll tell him to send you a box of candy."

She smiled cynically. "That'll be the day."

Retnick walked down to the Chinese laundry, playing a hunch; Evans hadn't used his room at night, which suggested a girl friend. And in that case he might have had his laundry sent to her place. The laundry man was small and young, with smooth blank eyes. Two children played behind the counter, and a woman in a shapeless dress and slippers was ironing shirts on a table against the wall. The room was warm and smelled cleanly of soap and fresh linen.

The young man remembered Evans. Yes. He had work shirts and dress shirts, lots of them. He dropped them off himself, usually in the morning, and his oldest boy delivered them. No, not down the block, but over on the east side.

Retnick's fingers were trembling slightly as he wrote down the address and apartment number.

"You a cop?" the young man asked him then.

Retnick smiled at him, letting him believe what he wanted, and the young man sighed and nodded. "Good job," he said.

Retnick thanked him and left. It was almost ten o'clock, the time he'd agreed to meet his wife at Tim Moran's. He hesitated on the cold, slushy sidewalk, staring at the address he had got from the laundryman. That would keep for a bit. The session with his wife wouldn't take long.

Five

Retnick walked into Tim Moran's saloon a few minutes after ten. The bar was crowded then with longshoremen who had been skipped over at the morning's shape-up. They were smoking and chatting over their beers, killing time until they could shape again in the afternoon. Several of them glanced curiously at Retnick as he moved to a vacant spot at the bar, his hands deep in the pockets of his overcoat. Tim Moran waved a greeting and came to meet him, a tentative smile touching his small red face.

"Has my wife been in here this morning?" Retnick said.

"I haven't seen her, Steve."

"I'll take a booth. Send her back, will you?"

"Sure. Can I bring you something to drink?"

"No, never mind."

Retnick walked to the rear of the big noisy room, moving down a narrow corridor formed by the crowded bar on his left and the line of brown wooden booths on his right. He hung up his hat and sat down in the last booth without bothering to take off his overcoat. From here he could see the length of the bar, the front doors and the big plate glass windows that faced the avenue. It was snowing again and the wind was higher. The big soft flakes rushed past in fast formations, straight lines of white against the windows.

Retnick lit a cigarette and stared at two longshoremen who were regarding him with simple curiosity. They turned

44

away, confused by the cold anger in his eyes, and they went back to their beer and talk. He settled down in the booth then and watched the smoke curling in slow spirals from his cigarette, isolated from the cheerful noises of the bar, by the dark and bitter cast of his thoughts. He glanced up when his wife came in. She closed the door quickly against the rush of cold air that swirled into the room, and stood indecisively for an instant, a small uncertain smile touching her lips. Her cheeks were flushed from the wind. She wore a gray tweed topcoat with a flaring skirt, and flakes of melting snow glistened in her close-cut, curly black hair. Moran saw her and waved, and she went to the bar and shook hands with him, moving with a quick light grace that seemed appropriate to any place or occasion. The men at the bar made room for her, grinning sympathetically as she stamped the snow from her small black pumps. There was a quality of direct, unself-conscious friendliness about her that put them completely at ease. A pretty picture, Retnick thought, staring impassively at her clean warm beauty. Charming the simple souls with a quick smile, a turn of a slim ankle. No wonder she looks good, he thought, putting out his cigarette. She's had five good years. Big good years. Anger twisted in his breast like the turn of a cold blade. She hadn't missed anything, anything at all.

She smiled at something Moran said in parting, and then walked quickly toward the rear of the room. But the smile left her face when Retnick stood up and she saw the look in his eyes; she faltered for an instant, as if a heavy weight had suddenly been placed on her shoulders.

"I'm sorry I'm late," she said, sliding into the booth. "There weren't any cabs. Have you been waiting long?"

The words meant nothing; they were defensive little flurries against the barrier in his face and eyes.

"It doesn't matter," he said. "What's on you mind?"

She was silent for a moment, frowning at the backs of her hands. Then she sighed and looked at him. "Last night was all wrong, Steve."

"What did you expect?"

"I thought we could talk to each other, at least."

"We talked," he said.

"We just made noisies," she said. "There was no more communication than you'd find between a Martian and a—a Zulu."

"Did that surprise you?"

She stared at him for a few seconds, studying the lines in his hard face. Then she said slowly, "Do you hate me so much you won't even listen to me? I want to explain what happened. Don't I deserve that much of a break?"

Retnick laughed shortly. "A break," he said. "That's very funny."

"It isn't funny," she said, with a sharp note of anger in her voice. "Who says I'm dirt on the floor? Who treats me like God's greatest slut? You, the final judge! But you won't listen to my side of it. You've made up your mind and the case is closed. I can go whistle."

Retnick lit a cigarette and flipped the match aside. "Is that all you've got to say?"

She put her hands over his suddenly. "I want a break and I don't deserve one. Is that so terrible? You've got to have some compassion left. They couldn't change you that much."

"I'm not interested in forgiving people," Retnick said.

She withdrew her hands from his slowly. "Forgiving your enemies isn't optional," she said. "It's something you've got to do. There's a direct order, isn't there? 'Father forgive them.' Or maybe that's not it. You could check with Father Bristow."

"I've got nothing to talk to him about," Retnick said.

"This is just a waste of time then," she said slowly.

Retnick's hands burned from the touch of her cool fingers. He swallowed a tightness in his throat and said, "Sure, it's a waste of time."

She looked down at the surface of the table and moistened her lips. For a moment she was silent. Then she said dryly, "That's that, I guess. If you want to play it like the great stone face, all right. What I wanted to talk to you about was this: I saved some money while you were gone. About six thousand dollars. I'd like you to take it and go away and do what you want with it. Go fishing or hunting, or go to Florida and lie in the sun, or get drunk for a year if you like. Then come back. Maybe we could talk by then. Would you do that, Steve?"

He smiled bitterly. "You think I'm that mixed up, eh? Like a G.I. with battle fatigue. Give him a few helpings of apple pie and let him loaf in the sun and he'll be okay."

"Then what *is* wrong with you?"

"Nothing's wrong with me," he said sharply. "I'm going to find the men who killed Ventra and there'll be a big, loud pay-off. That makes sense to me. If you don't think I'm right, then I suggest you take the dough and go on a therapeutic binge. You need it."

As he was talking Retnick heard the front door open and felt the sudden draft of cold air about his ankles. But he paid no attention to it until he became conscious of the strange, expectant silence that had settled over the room. He looked up then and saw Joe Lye and Hammy standing at the far end of the bar.

"Steve," she said. "Listen to me. I want—"

"I'll get you a cab," he said.

"Please. If you leave this way we can never fix it up."

"Let's go," he said, standing. "I don't want to talk any more."

She slipped from the booth, buttoning the collar of her coat, and Retnick picked up his hat. The longshoremen along the bar sipped beer in silence, minding their own business with scrupulous care. Tim Moran stood at the spigots, his face grave and impassive, but Retnick caught the little flash of warning in his eyes.

Marcia walked quickly toward the front door, her high heels sounding sharply in the unnatural stillness. Retnick followed her, ignoring the cautious glances shot at him by men at the bar. Then, when he was at the door, Joe Lye said, "Hello, Steve," and his voice fell softly into the silence.

Retnick hesitated. Marcia stopped with her hand on the

knob and looked up at him, suddenly aware of the tension in the room.

Lye said, "Don't hurry off because of us, Steve."

Retnick turned around slowly, hands deep in the pockets of his overcoat. Under the brim of his hat his face was expressionless. He knew it would be wise to clear out before there was trouble; but his control was slipping.

"What do you want, Joe?" he said quietly.

Lye and Hammy stood together at the turn of the bar, with space on either side of them; the men nearest them had drifted casually toward the juke box and lunch table at the rear of the room. Lye, tall and thin in black clothes, looked relaxed and easy, but the straining little smile was flashing like a danger signal at the side of his pallid face. Hammy was grinning expectantly. His hands were hooked onto the lapels of his tan overcoat, pulling it back from his huge chest. He looked slightly drunk; there was a hot gleam in his little eyes, and his round, flat face was flushed and beaded with perspiration.

The smile tightened on Lye's face. "There's some talk that you got dumb in jail," he said. "I wanted to check on that."

"How do you plan to find out?" Retnick said.

Lye laughed gently. "Well, maybe I'll give you one of those I.Q. tests. Hammy here can ask the questions."

Marcia caught Retnick's arm. "Steve, let's go."

"There's no hurry," he said, staring at Lye.

"They want trouble. Don't be a fool."

Hammy laughed happily. "Your wife says you're a fool and I guess she should know. How come you're living with a little kitty cat when you got a dish like that waiting for you, Retnick? That's the first question in the big I.Q. test."

The little grin on Retnick's lips did something ugly to his face. "I got questions too," he said. "Who killed Frank Ragoni? Who killed Joe Ventra? Those are mine, Joe. Tell Amato I'll be around to try them on him one of these days."

Lye's unnatural smile strained his mouth in a tight, twisted line. "You still talk real big, Steve. I bet Hammy can fix that."

"He can try," Retnick said gently.

"Steve, don't!" Marcia cried.

Hammy laughed again. "You big clown," he said, and surged toward Retnick, a long powerful arm swinging in an arc at his neck. He loved this work; all he needed was a grip and then he could maul and batter any man to pieces.

But he never got his grip; Retnick slapped his arm away with a blow that spun him around in a half-circle. Then he hit him twice in the body, deliberately and cruelly, bringing the punches up with effortless, terrible power, and Hammy's breath left his body in an agonized gasp. His hands dropped quickly, as if invisible weights had suddenly been shackled to his wrists, and he fought for breath through a wide, straining mouth. He stared at Retnick, his eyes bulging piteously, and Retnick hit him again, slugging the wide exposed jaw with all the strength in his body. Hammy's knees quit under him then, and he went down to the floor in a lugubrious sprawl, falling like an old man, limply and helplessly. Lying on his side, he panted for breath, a bloody froth bubbling on his lips.

Retnick stared at Joe Lye, who stood perfectly still, his face twisted into a fixed weird smile. "Do you still want to go on with your little question game?" he said softly. Already, the short, hot anger was gone, purged by the simple moment of action. But the old anger was with him still, cold and lasting, running powerfully under all his emotions.

Lye shook his head slowly. When he spoke his voice was barely audible. "It's your round."

"You're smart, Joe," Retnick said. The room was silent and still as he looked down at Hammy's helpless bulk. "Next time I'll kill you," he said. "Remember that."

Then he walked past his wife, opened the door and started uptown, moving with long strides into the driving snow. He heard her call his name and he heard her footsteps behind him, but he kept walking. She caught up with him finally and took his arm in both of her hands. "Steve, stop," she said. "Don't run away from me like this."

He looked down at her. She was very pale; her lipstick stood out as a vivid slash, and her eyes were dark with fear. "Why did you do it?" she said. "What's wrong with you?"

"They asked for it, they got it," he said.

"You wanted to kill him," she said. "Steve, you've got to stop. You're—you're like an animal."

"I'm not stopping. I haven't started yet."

She stared at him and then shook her head quickly. "It's not just me you hate. You hate everybody. You'll go on hating until you're killed."

"That shouldn't bother you," he said, and pulled his arm away from her and walked toward the avenue. She stared after him, one hand touching her throat, until his big body disappeared into the clouds of swirling snow.

Six

The building was a handsome brownstone in a quiet block east of Park, a street of neat iron grill-work and well-kept window boxes. The apartment number was 4 B, and the name on the tiny white card was Dixie Davis. This was where Red Evans had told the laundryman to deliver his shirts.

Retnick paused in the small lobby, smoothed down his thick black hair and brushed the snow from his shoulders. He pressed the buzzer then, knowing there was nothing to do but move ahead and hope for luck. Everything else was gone from his mind; his wife, Lye and Hammy, these were phantoms he could dissolve with an exercise of will. A tiny, scratching noise sounded from the speaker and a girl's voice said, "Hello?"

"This is a friend of Red Evans," he said. "I'd like to talk to you."

"Talk away, friend," she said indifferently; her voice sounded as if it hadn't registered surprise in a long, long time.

"I'd rather make it private. Can I come up for a minute?"

There was an interval of silence. Then she said, "Where'd you know Red?"

"At the docks. At the North Star Lines."

Again she hesitated. Then: "Okay, friend."

She stood in the doorway of her apartment, a small red-

51

head with very cold blue eyes. There was no interest or friendliness in her pale face; she studied him with instinctive caution as he walked down the short hallway from the landing. She was in her late twenties, he guessed, and nobody's innocent little doll. The sharp blue eyes, points of light under the red bangs, had seen more than their share of fakes and deadbeats and frauds.

He said, "I hope I'm not breaking up your schedule." She wore a blue silk robe and slippers, but her eyes and face were made up for the street.

She shrugged her thin shoulders, dismissing the apology as irrelevant. "When did you see Red last?" she said.

"Not for quite a while." Retnick glanced at the closed doors along the hall. "I'd rather not talk about it out here. It's pretty important."

· "Okay, come on in."

The room was small, but attractively furnished with conventional modern pieces. Everything was primly neat and clean; magazines formed orderly designs on the coffee tables, and the tiny felt pillows on the sofa were lined up as neatly as marshmallows in a box. The only personal note was a floppy Raggedy Ann doll which was propped up on an ottoman before the small television set.

"Mind if I smoke?" he said as she closed the door.

"Go ahead. What's so important about finding Red?"

"How about you?" He offered her the pack, but she shook her head and sat down in a deep chair beside a liquor cabinet. A door stood open behind her, and Retnick noticed an overnight bag on the bed and, beside it, a slip and nylon stockings. A pair of anklestrap sandals were placed neatly together on the floor. He lit his cigarette and glanced around for an ashtray.

"On the coffee table," she said.

"Thanks."

"Let's get on with it," she said. "Why'd you come here looking for Red?"

"I'll level with you," Retnick said. "I don't know Red. I never met the guy. But I want to find him."

She stared at him, one foot swinging slowly, her eyes shining and cold in her pale face. Then she said, "I don't go for jokers like you. What's your angle?"

"I want to find Evans. It's as simple as that."

"Are you a private cop or something?"

Retnick shook his head. "I just got out of jail. My name's Retnick. Does that mean anything to you?"

She shook her head slowly. "Should it?"

"Not particularly. Before I went up I gave some cash to a man I thought I could trust. A man by the name of Ragoni. Ever hear of him?"

"We must move in different crowds, friend," she said.

"You'll never meet Ragoni. He's dead," Retnick said. "He got killed about the time Red Evans disappeared from the docks. I learned that from some buddies of mine at the pier. I guess you see why I'm looking for Evans."

"You think maybe he's got your dough?"

Retnick smiled slightly. "It's worth checking, don't you think?"

"How'd you find out I knew him?"

"From his landlady. He gave her this address for forwarding mail."

"That's my redhead," she said, with a bitter little smile. "Give me one of those cigarettes, will you?"

"Sure." Retnick held a light for her and she murmured a thank you and let her head rest against the upholstered back of the chair. The bitter little smile was still on her lips. "So Red uses me as a forwarding address, eh? That's like him. He's a guy who takes over. And then he takes off. I can't help you, mister. I haven't heard from him since he walked out on me."

"That's too bad," Retnick said.

She laughed shortly. "It's the kindest thing he ever did. He took me for plenty, including what was left of my girlish dreams. I met him at the place I work, which is a saloon that calls itself a rendezvous. Okay, he's good-looking, and he's got a nice line. I buy it. Pretty soon he's moved in on me, which wasn't bad. We were a permanent deal, he said."

She smiled cynically and shook her head. "I'm believing all this, remember. We were going to Canada where everything was new and fresh. He wanted to raise cattle or something. You should hear him on the evils of cities. Corny, eh? Well, girls like corn, mister. It makes them fat and sleepy. One day he didn't show up, and I found three hundred dollars gone from my piggy bank." She spread her hands. "End of story. No Canada, no good life on the plains. If you find him, mister, you got my permission to use his head for a golf ball."

Retnick frowned slightly. "You think he might have gone to Canada alone?"

"I wouldn't know. He talked like he'd discovered the damn place, but he could have got all that from a book."

"Would you get in touch with me if he shows up again?"

She smiled at him, swinging one foot in a little circle. The silken robe slipped apart at her knees, revealing slender, chalk-white legs. "Was it a lot of money, mister?" she said slowly.

"It's enough for two people to have some fun with," Retnick said. "How about it?"

"You don't want to raise cattle and live the good life, by any chance?"

Retnick smiled and shook his head. "I'm a city type. I like my cattle with french-fries on the side. Do we do business?"

"So what can I lose?" she said. "If the bum shows up I'll let you know."

"Fine." Retnick took a pencil from his pocket and wrote his number on the back of a packet of matches. "You can get me there," he said, dropping the matches on the table. "And I know where to find you."

She stood and smoothed down the front of her robe. "This is a business deal, I think you said."

"That's right," Retnick said, smiling into her small hard eyes. "If you want to change the rules, let me know."

"Fair enough," she said, moving to the door. "Good luck, big boy."

"Thanks." Retnick walked past her into the short hallway and started down the stairs. When he heard her door close he stopped and listened to the silence for a moment or two. Then he went quietly back to her apartment and put his ear against the door. She was speaking to someone in a low, urgent voice, but he couldn't distinguish the words; her voice was a blur of anxious sound.

Retnick went down to the street then and walked a block before hailing a cab. "This is a tail job," he said to the driver. "Is that okay with you?"

The driver, an intelligent-looking old man, looked around at him. "Are you a cop?"

"I'm a husband," Retnick said. "Okay?"

"All right, get in," the old man said without enthusiasm.

Retnick lit a cigarette and settled back in the seat. From there he could see the entrance to Dixie's building. He felt reasonably certain that she was still in contact with Red Evans; her version of their relationship didn't fit her type. Things happened that way to some girls, but not to hard-shelled little characters like Dixie Davis.

She came out of her building about five minutes later and glanced at her watch as she started toward Park Avenue, picking her way awkwardly through the slush in high-heeled shoes.

"That your wife?" the driver said, shifting into first.

"Yes. Give her a little lead."

Dixie Davis crossed Park and stopped on the corner, obviously looking for a cab. "She's going downtown," Retnick said. "You'd better get ahead of her."

"I got you," the driver said. He swung into Park and stopped at the canopied entrance of an apartment building. The doorman came out from the lobby, but the driver held up a street-guide, and called, "Just checking an address, buddy."

The doorman nodded and went back to the lobby. In the rear-vision mirror Retnick saw Dixie climb into a cab that had pulled up for the red light. "Pick up the first Yellow that passes us," he told his driver.

"All right."

They followed the Yellow across town to the Pennsylvania station, and the driver said, "They're heading into the back tunnel. You want to go down?"

"Let a couple of cabs get ahead of us," Retnick said. When they stopped for a light he gave the driver a bill and waved the change.

"I hope this is where she told you she was going," the old man said, looking back at Retnick.

Retnick smiled slightly. "She's running true to form."

In the brightly lighted tunnel Retnick waited until Dixie had paid off her cab and started for the revolving doors that led to the station. Then he went down the ramp and signaled a Red Cap. "I've got a job for you," he said. "It's worth five bucks. Okay?"

"Sure, if it's legal," the Red Cap said.

"Come on with me." Inside the vast waiting room Retnick saw Dixie heading for the coach ticket windows. He pointed her out to the Red Cap and said, "Find out where she buys a ticket to. I'll wait here."

Retnick was able to follow Dixie's bright red hair through the crowd without difficulty. He saw her stop briefly at the ticket window, and then hurry toward the train shed with short quick steps. The Red Cap came back and said, "She's going to Trenton, sir. At least she bought a ticket there."

"Thanks very much," Retnick said, and gave him his money.

"Thank you, sir."

Trenton, Retnick thought, as he walked toward a rank of telephone booths. Was that where Red Evans had holed up? If so, one small part of the problem was solved. But the greater part remained: to establish who had paid him to do the job. Even then Retnick knew he might be no closer to the man who had killed Ventra. He was suddenly swept with a sense of oppressive futility. And when it was all over, when he had proved that a cop named Retnick had been framed, what the hell would it mean? Where would he be? Still sitting in a cheap bedroom, or standing at a cheap bar, as isolated from humanity as he was right now. For a moment or so he stared at the crowds passing him, experiencing a curious bitter loneliness. Some of the people looked happy. He wondered what they knew. Or what they didn't know. Finally he shrugged and stepped into a telephone booth. He called Kleyburg at the Thirty-First, and got through to him after a short wait. "You said to yell if I needed anything," he said.

"Sure, Steve. What is it?"

"Take this down." Retnick gave him Dixie Davis' name and address. Then he said, "I'd like to know all about her. Where she works, what her days off are, who she sees, and so forth. Is that possible?"

"I can manage it. She lives in the Twentieth, but I've got some friends over there. Between us we'll get a fix on her. Look, I'll have to cut this short. We're busy today." He hesitated, then said, "Maybe you haven't seen a paper."

"No, what's up?"

"They found old Jack Glencannon's body a couple of hours ago. On a siding just off Twelfth Avenue."

"What happened to him?"

"Nobody's sure yet. But it looks like a homicide."

Retnick sat in the booth for a moment or so, staring at the bustle and commotion in the cavernous station. There was a hard little smile on his lips. This would tighten the screws on Nick Amato, whether he was responsible for the old man's death or not. The papers would set fires under the cops and unions now. The pot would boil and the public would want a victim or two tossed into it. That was fine. Let them all burn.

Seven

At four o'clock that afternoon Retnick stood watching the entrance to the North Star Lines terminal. It was almost dark then; the snow had stopped falling but a damp heavy fog swirled in massive clouds off the river. Floodlights, mounted on the piers, picked up shifting gleams on the surface of the water, and the moan of fog horns was a threatening sound above the rumble of traffic. Retnick smoked one cigarette after another, and kept his eyes on the entrance to the North Star Lines. Finally the little Irishman, Grady, appeared, leaving work with a group of longshoremen. This was the man Retnick wanted to talk to, Grady, the winchman whose job Red Evans had taken over. The men crossed the street, their figures black and clumsy in the gray fog, heading for the welcoming yellow gleam of Tim Moran's saloon. When they disappeared inside Retnick lit another cigarette and settled down to wait.

It was six when Grady came out of Moran's. He was alone now, and his step was brisk but slightly unsteady as he started uptown.

Retnick followed him through the darkness for a block or two and came up behind him in an empty stretch of the avenue. He put a hand on Grady's arm and crowded him against the brick wall of a warehouse. "I've been looking for you, Grady," he said.

Grady was slightly drunk and he didn't quite understand

what was happening. "What's the matter with you now?" he said, blinking at Retnick. "Let me by. What kind of funny business are you pulling?"

"I was a friend of Frank Ragoni's," Retnick said.

"Sure we were all his friends," Grady said. His mood changed and he sighed. "It was a dirty shame, a dirty shame. Him with a family and everything." He stared up at Retnick, a frown twisting his small, flushed face. "You were at the pier this morning, weren't you?" he said. "You're Retnick."

"That's right. I want some answers. You got sick and Evans took your job. Did somebody tell you to get sick?"

Grady shook his head quickly. "No, it's God's truth I had the flu. I couldn't get out of me bed."

"And while you were sick Red Evans took your winch," Retnick said. "That's right, isn't it?"

"Yes, that's right," Grady said, nodding vigorously.

"And Evans dropped a load on Ragoni. It missed by an inch. That's right, isn't it?"

Grady shrugged and smiled weakly. "I wasn't there, you know. But that's what I heard." He looked up and down the dark street, wetting his lips. "My old lady is waiting supper for me. I'd best be going."

"Don't be in a hurry," Retnick said. "Do you know why I went to jail?"

"Well, they said you killed a man, but I never put any stock in that."

"Put some stock in it," Retnick said staring into Grady's watery blue eyes. "Why did you stay off the job?"

"It was the flu, I told you."

"Will you stick to that when the cops get to you?"

Grady looked up at Retnick and a strange fear claimed him completely. He began to breathe rapidly. "They told me not to shape for a week," he said, catching hold of Retnick's hands. "They said I'd get myself killed."

"Was the hiring boss in on it? And Brophy?"

"I don't know, I swear to God. Nobody talks about it."

"Amato is ready to take over your local, eh?"

"It'd be worth your life to stand up to them now," Grady

said, glancing anxiously up and down the dark street. "Old Union Jack, himself, is dead, you know. Happened today. Who knows who'll be next? Hah! Ask Joe Lye. Or Hammy. Or Dave Cardinal. They can tell you maybe." Grady smiled shakily, trying to coax sympathy into Retnick's bitter eyes. "I—I didn't feel good about laying up pretending to be sick. I knew they were after somebody. But what could I do? A man can't stand up alone to them killers, can he? My boy is in the army, and they'd be no one to look after the old lady if something happened to me. You see how it was, don't you?"

"Sure, it never changes," Retnick said shortly. "Who was it told you to stay home? Which one of them?"

"That was Mario."

"Mario?"

"Nick Amato's nephew. He's a punk, but he's got them others behind him."

"Go on home," Retnick said. "Enjoy your dinner."

"What else could I do?" Grady said, staring guiltily into Retnick's dark hard face. "What else could I do?"

Retnick turned without answering him and walked into the darkness. Now he had two names: Mario Amato and Red Evans. It was a good bet that Mario had engineered the execution. If that were true, if young Mario had hired Red Evans, they would have to be thrown together under pressure. One of them might crack. Not Evans, who was probably a cold and tough professional, but young Mario was another matter; Retnick remembered him as a boy of seventeen, weak and petulant, vain about his looks and clothes, getting by on his uncle's reputation. Now he would be twenty-three, Retnick thought. A tough boy, doing man-sized jobs for Amato, arranging murders like an old hand. Retnick smiled coldly into the darkness. We'll see how tough he is, he was thinking . . .

Retnick ate a lonely dinner that night, savoring his dark thoughts like a miser. They were all he had, these bitter anticipations of vengeance, and he didn't realize how dear they had become to him; he lived in a sense on anger, and he hadn't thought very much about what he would be when his anger was fully satisfied.

When he finished dinner he walked uptown on Broadway, going all the way to Harlem, barely noticing the people and streets he passed. Then he turned around and came back downtown, with no destination in mind, but only hoping to tire himself enough to sleep. At nine-thirty he stopped in front of the Gramercy Club staring at his wife's picture, which was in a glass panel to one side of the entrance. It had been taken a long time ago, shortly after they were married; her hair had been long then, brushed down to her shoulders in a page-boy, and her eyes were bright with careless happiness. Retnick studied the picture for a full minute, tracing the soft curve of her lips with his eyes.

Finally he turned away and walked slowly toward the corner, staring at the bright busy street, and the cheerful-looking people coming in and out of bars and restaurants. Snow was falling again, softly and lightly; the wind had died away and the bright flakes fell in slow straight lines, gleaming prettily in the colored light from neon signs. Retnick stopped, confused by his feelings and walked back to the Gramercy. He went inside and took a seat at the bar, not bothering to check his hat and coat. The bartender remembered him and said hello.

"It was whisky with water, I believe," he said.

"That's fine," Retnick said, staring across the dining room at his wife. She was playing an old show tune, lightly and stylishly, smiling down at the keyboard. A light behind her threw her face in the shadows; he could only see the soft gleam of her lips.

The bartender leaned toward him and said, "Do you want me to send word to her that you're here?"

Retnick rubbed a hand over his forehead. "No, never mind." Standing abruptly he started toward the door. He had to wait an instant to let a group of people come in, and it was then, as he glanced once more at his wife, that he noticed a dark-haired man sitting alone at a table that faced the piano. The light was uncertain, soft and hazy with cigarette smoke, but Retnick was able to pick out the man's features, the heavy lips, the dark full eyebrows. He hesitated a second or two, frowning, and then walked back to the bar. When the bartender came over to him Retnick pointed out the man, and asked if he were a regular customer.

"Not a regular, certainly," the bartender said thoughtfully. "This is the first time I've noticed him."

"Okay, thanks," Retnick said. Outside he crossed the street and stood where he could watch the entrance of the Gramercy Club. The man watching his wife with such interest was Davey Cardinal, one of Amato's enforcers.

It was an hour later that Cardinal strolled out of the club and waved to a cab. He was short and stockily built, with the manners of a show-off; he played to an audience always, delighting in his role of tough guy. But behind this childish, arrogant façade, Retnick knew he was extremely shrewd and ruthless. Watching the tail light of his cab winking into the darkness, Retnick began to frown. His concern was blended of anger and exasperation; it wouldn't do them any good to strike at him through Marcia. But they didn't know that.

When he got to his room that night he found a note from Mrs. Cara under his door. Sergeant Kleyburg had called and asked if Retnick would stop by his home in the morning. Around eight.

Eight

Miles Kleyburg lived alone in a small apartment a few blocks from Yorktown. His wife had died in childbirth leaving him two sons to look after. But they too were gone now. One had married and moved to California to live, and the other had chosen the army as a career and was presently stationed in Germany.

Retnick knew all about the boys; he had served as the chief outlet for Kleyburg's parental pride during the years they had worked together as partners. Then he had sympathized with the old man's loneliness. Now he knew that it was an inescapable factor of existence. Everybody's alone, he was thinking, as he rang the bell to Kleyburg's apartment. The sooner people learned that, the better off they were. But it was a bitter truth, and they fought against it. They wanted to belong to someone, anyone at all, and they closed their eyes to the fact that they were nakedly alone. They went through ritualistic rites pretending the opposite was true, making faith a hostage against loneliness and betrayal. Trusting their friends, repeating words like love and honor to their brides before solemn altars, believing out of fear in someone who was all-kind, all-loving, all-powerful. And, to that someone, they made the most pathetic commitments of all, because they thought they could belong to him fovever. But none of it was true, none of it signified any-

63

thing. I know, he thought, and felt a bitter sterile pride in his knowledge.

Kleyburg opened the door and grinned as he put out his hand. "Well, it's good to see you," he said. "Come on in."

"Did you get a line on Dixie Davis?" Retnick said, as he entered the warm, clean living room.

"I think I got what you need," Kleyburg said. "Go on, take off your coat. We're not heading for a fire." Kleyburg was freshly shaved, and wore an old jacket and a pair of slacks. "I'm off duty today and I thought we could sit around a while and chew the rag. After we chew up some breakfast. How about it?"

Retnick took out his cigarettes and said, "I'm in a hurry, Miles. What about the girl?"

"Sure, if that's the way you want it." Kleyburg ran a hand over his gray hair and smiled awkwardly. He looked old and tired, Retnick thought. "Remember, though, how we used to come up here for breakfast sometimes after finishing the twelve-to-eight shift? I thought we could do it like that. Come on, Steve, I've got fresh sausages and fresh eggs on tap. How about it? You look like you could use a solid meal."

"I'll have coffee if it's ready," Retnick said. "The big breakfast will have to wait."

Kleyburg was obviously disappointed. "Okay, Steve," he said, shrugging and smiling. "Sorry I can't sell you the whole menu though. Sit down, I'll get the coffee."

When he left Retnick lit a cigarette and glanced around the room. The place had a comfortable, cluttered look to it. Sports magazines, pipes, a couple of big reading chairs, and the pictures of the boys on the mantel. Dozens of pictures, ranging from large tinted portraits to informal snapshots. The soldier boy, his silver bars agleam, stared solemnly into the future from one end of the mantel, while opposite him his brother stood tall and erect in a wedding picture with his bride. There were snaps of the married couple in California, lounging in shorts in the sun, and several of the soldier boy preparing for his trade. Sighting over a forty-five, posing on the turret of a tank, lying in the prone position with a rifle tucked expertly under his chin.

Kleyburg came in with the coffee and said, "Here we are!" Then he smiled at the pictures of his sons. "They're doing okay, don't you think?"

"They look good," Retnick said. He took a cup of coffee and sat down on the edge of the couch. There should be something else to say, he thought. Kleyburg obviously expected it; this was like old times for him, relaxing after a night's work, bragging inoffensively about his kids. But these weren't old times for Retnick, and he hadn't the warmth or interest to pretend they were. "How about the girl?" he said.

"I got a break on her," Kleyburg said, changing his tone to match Retnick's. "Nielsen at the Twentieth had her up on a charge a few months ago. Her name is Dorothy not Dixie, but the last name is honest. She works at an Eighth Avenue clipjoint. Nielsen arrested her and a few others like her on a Navy complaint. Seems the girls were taking the gobs for everything but their gold fillings, and the Navy asked us to look into it. Dixie's twenty-nine and she's been in and out of trouble. Shoplifting, hustling, con games, you name it. Dixie takes off two days a week, Tuesday and Thursday." Kleyburg shrugged. "That's about it, Steve."

"No line on her boy friends?"

Kleyburg shook his head. "She's the Navy's friend."

"Any mention of a guy name Red Evans?"

"I gave you all Nielsen gave me, Steve."

"Does that name mean anything to you?"

"Red Evans? Nothing in particular. Why?"

There was no humor in Retnick's smile. "I'm looking for him," he said, standing.

"Hold it a second," Kleyburg said, frowning at the bitter smile on Retnick's lips. "I want to say something to you. I was awake most of the night thinking about it, and I want to get it off my chest." He paused and took a deep breath. "You're on a downhill slide, boy, and you'll end in a crash. You've got reason to be mad. Sure. But you can choke on hate easier than you can a fishbone. I know. I know because I felt that way when my wife died. I thought I'd got a kick in the teeth from the whole world. And you can't live feeling like that."

Retnick shrugged. "I'm alive, Miles."

"Now wait," Kleyburg said, shaking his head. "I want to finish. If I get sidetracked I'll never get this said. When my wife died I hated everybody. I didn't even want the kids. But I couldn't walk away from my responsibility. It would have been easy to give the kids away; my sister was itching to get her hands on them. But I stuck it out, and it was no fun doing the job alone. And this is what I want to tell you, I guess. Lots of people helped me over those tough times. My mother-in-law took care of the kids until I got a housekeeper, and neighbors came in with all kinds of assistance, and even my house sergeant, the old crab, Bill Rafferty, gave me details close to home so I could duck in and see that everything was going all right. Most people are decent, Steve. They'll help you over this trouble. Don't go on thinking everybody is rotten."

"I'm not interested in people," Retnick said. "I'm interested in the men who framed me. Nobody else matters."

"You'll ruin yourself," Kleyburg said, making a futile gesture with his hand. "You were a fine decent guy, Steve. You had sympathy for everybody. Remember how you listened to me talk about the boys? You probably won't realize what that meant until you have some kids of your own."

Retnick wished the old man would stop talking so that he could leave, but Kleyburg went on, moving his hands about in anxious little flurries. "I've got to make you understand what I'm saying," he said. "Look, I was never the cop you were. I didn't have the brains and the drive. You carried me. I know that. You walked into trouble, you went through doorways first, and into dark alleys, and I held down the radio in the car. You think that didn't mean anything to me? That's why I can't stand by and let you wreck your life."

The words didn't touch Retnick; they were noises that

meant nothing. "Don't worry about me," he said. "I'll take care of myself."

"It isn't a matter of just living or dying," Kleyburg said, shaking his head stubbornly. "It's how you live and die, Steve. I'm an old man, and I understand some things better than you can. You've got to live in peace. You've got to forgive people. You've—"

"Stop it," Retnick said abruptly. "You're getting comical." Kleyburg put a hand on his arm, but Retnick pulled away from him and turned to the door. "Save your sermon. I don't need it."

At seven o'clock that night Retnick walked into the west side funeral home where Union Jack Glencannon would receive his last mortal respects. He had spent most of the day making a cautious effort to get on young Mario Amato's trail; but so far without luck. Now he checked the register of names at the door, knowing that Mario would probably show up at the wake. That was protocol on the docks; everyone went to funerals. But Mario hadn't made his visit yet.

Retnick signed his name on the mourners' page and walked into the thickly carpeted chapel, which was heavy with the scent of flowers. The place wasn't crowded; two men he didn't know stood before the casket and a third was wandering along the ranks of massed floral pieces inspecting the names of the donors.

Glencannon looked sad and stern in death, his big bold face incongruous against the quilted lining of the coffin. Beside him lay the scabbard and sword of the Knights of Columbus, and a worn Rosary was intertwined about his heavy hands. Instinctively Retnick crossed himself and said a prayer. The words came back effortlessly, which surprised him; it had been so long since he had prayed for anyone.

Leaving the chapel, he found a secluded chair in the adjoining room from where he could watch the foyer. There were half-a-dozen men sitting about in this room, talking in low voices and filling the air with smoke from pipes and cigars.

The crowd began to arrive an hour or so later. It was a solemn and important occasion, and it brought out top officials from the city, the unions and industry. The mayor stayed almost an hour and that word was passed with quiet pride to later arrivals. There was a steady stream of cops, firemen and longshoremen, friends of the old man's for nearly half a century. And with these came shipping executives, railroad men, heads of the various firms that sprawled along the waterfront.

Retnick saw Nick Amato and Joe Lye when they came in around ten o'clock. Amato wore a bulky brown overcoat and smiled at people he knew like an eager-to-please fruit peddler. Only his eyes gave him away; they reflected his cynical contempt for this exhibition.

Lye stayed behind Amato, his eyes quick and alert in his tense face; he carried his body as if it were a ticking bomb, a thin black cylinder of potential destruction. It was this strange explosive quality about Lye that made him feared and hated along the waterfront. And it was no act. He didn't play at being a toughie like Dave Cardinal. The dangerous pressures inside him were nakedly apparent in his pale eyes and queer straining lips.

The night wore on. The five Antuni brothers arrived, dignified, rather courtly men who ruled five thousand longshoremen in Jersey with hands of steel, and who feared nothing in the world except their youngest brother, a priest on Staten Island. The crowd kept coming, ex-fighters, cops, newspapermen, dockworkers, saloon keepers, union officials, hoodlums, and politicians. But there was no sign of young Mario Amato.

Retnick was putting out a tasteless cigarette when Lieutenant Neville drifted over to him and said, "Who're you waiting for, Steve?"

Retnick hadn't seen him come in. He said, "No one. Why?"

"Don't kid me. You haven't taken your eyes off the front door. Who're you expecting?"

"Mario Amato."

"What's your interest in him?"

Retnick shrugged. "Let's say it's personal."

Lieutenant Neville lit a cigarette and stared thoughtfully at the glowing tip. There was a puzzled expression on his lean intelligent face. "What's the point of being cozy with me, Steve?" he said. "We're after the same thing, but your way is wrong. I told you yesterday to keep out of trouble."

"Am I in trouble?" Retnick said, looking at him evenly.

"That fight with Hammy was a pretty stupid business."

"He wanted it, I didn't."

"It gave Amato a chance to gripe," Neville said. "Not to me, but downtown. I get the repercussions. He doesn't want a labor-hating ex-con roaming around the docks beating up his boys."

"Labor hating," Retnick said. "That's good."

"So I have an official order to keep an eye on you."

"That must make you feel fine," Retnick said. "Getting orders relayed to you from that hoodlum."

"I don't want to argue about it," Neville said.

"Thanks a lot," Retnick said. "Now we can move to important considerations. Such as who killed old man Glencannon. And Frank Ragoni."

Neville ignored the bitterness in Retnick's voice. "The lab isn't sure about Glencannon," he said. "It could be a homicide, or it could be a natural death. He went to Amato's office around midnight, and Amato says he was in good shape when he left. He was found a dozen blocks from there yesterday, behind a string of gondolas on a storage siding."

Retnick grinned coldly. "You want some advice? Arrest Nick Amato for the murder."

"We aren't calling it a murder yet," Neville said. Spots of color had come up in his pale cheeks. "Glencannon was an old man. His heart could have quit on him. The bruise on his head could have resulted from the fall. He could have crawled to where he was found."

"That's very logical," Retnick said dryly. "Or he might have been hit by lightning, or died laughing at old jokes. Investigate those angles, too. But don't bother Nick Amato.

He's too busy planning his next murder."

Neville said coldly, "I'm getting fed up with you, Steve. You think you're a lonely tragic figure who's been wronged by everybody in the whole world. That may fatten up your ego but it's lousy logic."

"You don't get logical in jail," Retnick said. He was starting to say something else when he noticed Mario Amato moving through the thinning crowd with two young men about his own age. He was slim and dark, with soft brown eyes, and he walked with a little swagger, as if he were certain that everyone in the room knew who he was, and was staring at him with interest and respect. He wore a beautifully fitted topcoat and carried a white fedora. Smiling broadly, he seemed in high spirits, obviously delighted to be leaving this place of gloom and death.

When he had passed through the doors Retnick said, "I've got to go, lieutenant."

"Yes, I guess you do," Neville said wearily. He had seen Mario, too, and his eyes were troubled as he watched Retnick crossing the floor, moving with the deliberate stride of a hunter.

Nine

Mario Amato stopped at the avenue with his two companions and tried to decide how to spend the rest of the evening. It was cold and windy on the corner and he pulled the collar of his fancy overcoat up tight about his throat. The traffic was light and the sidewalks were empty. Ahead of them the neon signs of bars winked invitingly into the black tunnel of the street. But he didn't feel like drinking; liquor had never had much appeal to him. A girl would be more like it. He wanted to forget the look of Glencannon's face, and the heavy depressing scent of the flowers. A girl would do that.

Retnick came silently from the darkness behind him and put a big hand on his arm. "I've been looking for you," he said.

Mario started nervously. "What the hell's the idea?" he said in a high, angry voice. One of his companions surged forward, but Retnick struck him across the chest with a forearm that was like a bar of iron, and the young man backed off quickly, gasping for breath. "Keep out of this," Retnick said. The two young men stared at him, breathing hard, checked by the look in his face.

Mario tried to pull free but Retnick's hand was like an iron collar about his arm. "What's the idea?" he said again, but plaintively now. "I don't know you, Mac."

"Tell me you don't know my sister."

71

Mario smiled weakly. What he saw in Retnick's eyes made him very nervous. "I don't think I know your sister," he said. "Maybe I met her somewhere. What's her name?"

"Nancy Riordan. And you aren't running out on her, get that straight."

"Look, mister, I don't know anybody by that name."

"I want to hear you tell her that," Retnick said. "Come on, let's go."

"Now wait a minute," Mario cried.

"That's Nick Amato's nephew," one of his friends said. "You better be sure what you're doing."

Retnick stared at him. "You mean he's too good for my sister?"

The young man shrugged and tried to smile. "No, I just thought I'd tell you."

"Well, don't bother telling me things," Retnick said. "You guys aren't involved in this. But you will be if you keep shooting off your mouths. I'll deal you in for free."

Both young men shook their heads quickly. "It's between you and him," one of them said.

"Fine. Beat it."

"Sure, we were going." They nodded jerkily to Mario. "See you around," one of them said. Mario stared wistfully after them as they hurried off, their heads pulled down into the collars of their coats. There was no one else in sight. Not even a cop. The city was dark and empty.

"Mister, you got me wrong," he said, smiling uncertainly at Retnick. "I never treated any girl wrong, I swear."

"That's what we're going to make sure of," Retnick said. "Maybe you're not the guy. If so, there's no harm done. Let's walk. She's waiting for us a few blocks from here. . . ."

Retnick unlocked his room, ushered Mario in ahead of him and closed the door. When he snapped on the lights the little cat blinked at them from the bed. It yawned and stretched a paw tentatively into the air.

"What's the gag?" Mario said, looking around with a worried smile.

Retnick tossed his coat on the bed and unloosened his tie. "Sit down, Mario," he said. "You know Red Evans, I guess."

"Yeah, I know him," Mario said slowly.

"We're going to talk about him," Retnick said, walking toward young Amato. "Sit down, I told you."

"Yeah, but your sister—"

"There's no sister," he said, and shoved Mario into a straight-backed chair. Standing over him, his eyes bright and hard, Retnick said, "There's just you and me, sweetheart. We're going to talk about how much you paid Evans to murder Frank Ragoni."

Mario wet his lips and tried desperately to keep the fear inside him from showing in his face. He was no stranger to violence, but not at these odds. As Nick Amato's nephew he lived in a cocoon of security and privilege. He had never faced trouble alone; his uncle's men saw to that.

"I don't know what you're talking about," he said, putting what strength he could muster into his voice. "You got me all wrong, I tell you."

"Where did you know Evans?"

"Well, around the docks. Just to say hello to. You know how it is?" He tried to meet Retnick's eyes directly, but it was almost impossible; there was something in them that was like the frightening stillness in old Glencannon's face. "I wasn't a friend of his," he went on anxiously. "We just nodded to each other, that's all."

Retnick stared at him in silence. Then he said quietly, "We won't have any trouble if you tell the truth, Mario. I know you hired Evans to do the job on Ragoni. I got that from the winchman, Grady. Did your uncle tell you to hire Evans? That's what I want to know."

"You got no right to accuse me of being a murderer," Mario said. He was becoming excited now and some of his fear left him. "You're asking for real trouble, buddy. I'm no punk you can push around."

He started to get up but Retnick put a hand against his chest and slammed him back into the chair. "I told you to sit down," he said, smiling unpleasantly. "Why did your uncle want Ragoni killed?"

Mario's breath came unevenly; he was suddenly close to tears. "I don't know anything about it," he said. "Somebody gave you the wrong dope on me."

Retnick knew he was lying; fear and guilt were stamped on him like a brand. For an instant he debated the wisdom of knocking the truth out of him; it wouldn't be hard. This was a punk, a pretty boy with soft nervous eyes and skin like a girl's. He'd be hopping bells or jerking sodas if it weren't for his uncle. But Retnick decided against force. Amato could toss him to the parole board.

Turning away he took out his cigarettes. "You can beat it," he said. "We'll have another talk one of these days."

Mario stood up and edged nervously past Retnick to the door. "You got me wrong, I'm telling you."

"You're in trouble, sonny," Retnick said. "And your uncle can't fix it. Tell him a guy by the name of Retnick told you that."

When Mario had gone Retnick locked the door and sat down on the edge of the bed. The cat curled up beside him and closed its eyes. Retnick stroked her absently and she began to purr. Frowning through the smoke of his cigarette, he tried to guess what was coming. Trouble, of course. Mario would run squealing to his uncle and that would start it. But there was no other way to play it. He had to push until something started to give.

Ten

Nick Amato listened to his nephew's story as he sipped black coffee in the kitchen of his west side cold-water flat. The kitchen was the only room in which he felt comfortable. His wife had filled the rest of the house with holy pictures, dull heavy furniture, and retouched portraits of her relatives in Naples. And everything smelled of furniture polish.

Amato was in shirtsleeves, with his elbows on the table and a cup of coffee cradled in his hands. He was mad, and getting madder every minute, but he kept the musing little smile on his lips. Joe Lye sat at the end of the table watching Mario, and Hammy, a bandage along his right cheek and jaw, stood in the corner, twisting his hat around in his hands and breathing noisily through his damaged nose.

"So that's all," Amato said, staring with cold brown eyes at his coffee cup. "You haven't forgot nothing, eh?"

"I told you just the way it happened," Mario said, rubbing his damp forehead. He was frightened by his uncle's reaction; if Amato had laughed or cursed he would have felt better. Maybe the big guy, Retnick, knew something. *You're in trouble your uncle can't fix!* That's what he'd said.

"So that's all," Amato said. "He asked you about Evans and Ragoni and you told him nothing. Is that it?"

"I swear that's all," Mario said. "I told you about him hitting me and the rest of it."

"Yeah," Amato said. He looked up at his nephew, staring

at him as he would stare at a bug crawling on his plate. "Did you hit him back? I forget."

"What could I do?" Perspiration shone on Mario's face, dampened the little curls of hair along his temples. "He might have killed me."

"Retnick?" Amato laughed softly. "Don't worry about him." He turned to Hammy. "He's not tough. Ain't that right, Hammy?"

"I was drunk," Hammy said. He shifted his great weight from one foot to the other, and smiled stupidly at Amato. The beating from Retnick had effected a change in him; the dumb trust in himself was gone, and his eyes were sheepish and puzzled. "I was drunk," he said again. "He caught me when I was fouled up from drinking."

"You'll get him the next time, eh?" Amato said, staring at the shame in his eyes. Like a castrated bull, Amato thought. "Next time, eh."

Hammy smiled as if this were a joke; he wanted no more of Retnick. The memory of those blows to his body was frighteningly vivid; another one would have killed him, he knew. "Sure, Nick," he said, laughing nervously.

"Next time he'll kill you," Amato said, knowing what was going on in Hammy's mind. "Remember that."

A soft knock sounded on the door. Amato looked around irritably and called out, "Yeah?"

His wife entered the room smiling an apology at Amato. She was stout and middle-aged, with a dark complexion and large brown eyes. Her black dress, shapeless and old, fell almost to her ankles, and she wore her gray hair in a large bun at the back of her neck. There was a heavy resignation in her manner, but it didn't stem from peace of mind or calmness of soul; instead she looked as if she had signed an armistice with life before a shot could be fired.

She stood close to Mario, almost touching him, and said to her husband, "He's upset and tired, Nick. Can't he go to bed?"

"Sure, he can go to bed," Amato said, drumming his fingers on the table. Once he had seen a blasphemous picture of a cow saying a rosary and the image nagged at him when he looked at his wife.

"I did all I could," Mario said, making a last attempt to alter the ominously hard expression around his uncle's lips.

"Go to bed," Amato said. "Don't worry about it."

His wife shepherded Mario from the room and before the door closed Amato heard her promising to bring him some warm milk with a little brandy in it. Amato put down his cup and swore softly.

Hammy, guessing at the source of his irritation, nodded solemnly and said, "That kid will turn out spoiled, I bet. Anna's too good to him."

"Joe, give Hammy a thousand dollars," Amato said.

Lye hesitated, smiling uncertainly; the request made no sense but he knew Amato was in one of his dangerous, unpredictable moods.

Amato suddenly pounded his fist on the table. Glaring at Lye, he said, "You want to know what for? You want to vote on things maybe, be democratic?"

"Hell no, Nick," Lye said hastily. He counted out ten one hundred dollar bills from his wallet and handed them to Hammy.

"What's this for?" Hammy said, staring in confusion at the money.

"That's your severance pay," Amato said, getting to his feet.

"Wait a minute, you can't—"

"Shut up!" Amato yelled at him. He crouched slightly, as if the weight of his anger was more than he could bear, and Lye moved slowly to the wall and covered Hammy with the gun in his overcoat pocket.

"You killed old man Glencannon," Amato said, in a low thick voice.

"I didn't mean to," Hammy said, shaking his head desperately. "I just cuffed him and he—well he fell over."

"You're lucky I'm letting you quit," Amato said, pounding a fist on the kitchen table. "What'll it look like when I take over his local next month? The International can move in and call the election a phony. The papers are going to have a lot to say about hoodlums and killers on the docks. Sure, but that doesn't mean anything to you." Amato paused, breathing heavily, bringing his anger under control. "There's five hundred men in my local who do what I tell 'em to do. I say work, they work; I say strike, they strike. But you got to be different, you got to do things on your own."

"Boss, I was trying to make him wait for a cab," Hammy said, rubbing his big hands together nervously. His little eyes were wide and frightened. "He pulled away from me, and I grabbed him. Maybe I hit him. But not hard. And he just fell over. I—I dumped him then. That was all I could do. You got to give me a break."

"You're getting a break," Amato said coldly. "I could turn you over to the cops. But I'm letting you go. But I want you to go fast, understand? Get out of town and stay out."

Hammy looked desperately puzzled and hurt, like a child whose values had been ridiculed by a trusted adult.

"This ain't a fair shake," he said at last. "It's because of that Polack, Retnick. You think I'm no good because he dropped me. I told you I was drunk."

Lye said softly, "You're crowding your luck, Hammy. You heard Nick. Don't let me see you in New York again."

Hammy looked away from Lye's fixed and deadly smile. He knew what that smile meant. "I'm going," he said wetting his lips. "I ain't mad."

"I'll see you to the door," Lye said. "Then I don't want to see you again anywhere."

When Lye returned to the kitchen, Amato was seated at the kitchen table puffing on a cigar. "Has Retnick got a phone?" he said, looking up at Lye through the ropy layers of smoke.

"Yeah. There's one in his boarding house."

"Call him up and tell him I want to see him. Right away. Here."

"You think he'll come?"

Amato shrugged. "Sure. That's why he roughed up the kid."

"You should let me handle him now," Lye said. "He's trouble, Nick. And he's getting help from the boys at the Thirty-First."

"Go call him up," Amato said. "I don't want any more loud bangs along my stretch of the docks. You call him."

"Okay, Nick."

While Lye was out of the room his wife came in and put a saucepan of milk on the stove to heat. The kitchen was crowded with equipment, all of it gleaming and new. Anna seemed at home among these mechanical marvels. They were a big thing to her, Amato knew. Mario, the church and the kitchen. That was her life. He watched her, frowning slightly, as she took down a large breakfast cup and measured out two tablespoonfuls of brandy into it. Then she stirred the steaming milk slowly, and a little smile touched her full patient lips.

"For the kid?" Amato asked her.

She nodded, without looking at him; her attention was claimed by the simmering milk. "He's upset," she said.

"He'll be okay."

Anna poured the milk into the cup and put the saucepan back on the stove. Then she turned and looked at her husband. There was a curiously cold expression on her dark face. "He told me a man hit him tonight," she said. "Can't you keep him safe?"

"Things like that happen. They don't mean nothing."

"This mustn't happen to him, Nick. He's all I got. You know that."

"Sure, sure," Amato said irritably. Most of the time he was glad he'd arranged to have Mario shipped to America. But there were moments when he wished he'd let him rot in Naples. The boy gave Anna something to think about besides polishing the furniture and hanging around the church. That part was fine; but her simple-minded anxiety about him was a bore. Amato had bought little Mario the way

he'd buy an ice box or a suit of clothes; they had no kids
and Anna cried about it at night, so he got her sister to ship
them her oldest boy, Mario. That was fifteen years ago,
and since then Anna had lived for the boy, coddling and
smothering him with her frustrated maternal longings.

"I'll take care of him," Amato said, hoping to end the
matter.

"He's not strong like other boys," Anna said. "He's not
rough and wild. He should make something out of himself.
It's no good that he works with your men. He should be a
priest or a teacher." Anna spoke with dogged insistence, as
if emphasis alone might make her dreams come true.

Amato puffed on his cigar, avoiding her eyes. The cow
with the rosary, he was thinking. The idea of Mario as a
priest or teacher—or anything at all for that matter—struck
him as slightly absurd. "Don't worry about him," he said.
"He'll be okay."

"I try not to worry," she said. "You don't know how hard
I try." Then she left the room without looking at him and
went quickly down the hallway to her ''son.''

Lye returned in a moment or so and sat down at the end
of the table. "I talked to him," he said. "He'll come."

Amato grunted and puffed on his cigar. His mood had
turned sour and bitter. He wouldn't have admitted it, but
Anna's jealous preoccupation with Mario made him feel
unimportant. "You seeing that broad of yours tonight?" he
asked Lye.

"It's pretty late," Lye said, trying to be casual about it.

"Can't you answer a simple question?" Amato said. "I
know it's late. I got a watch, too."

"Yeah, I'll see her, I guess," Lye said.

"You got a nice life," Amato said, staring at Lye. "Martinis and steaks, real high style." The thought of Kay Johnson
made him restless and irritable; he had never seen her apartment but he imagined it as a place of soft lights and deep
chairs, with music playing, maybe, and lots of good liquor
in crystal decanters. And he saw her there, very pale and
blonde, with white shoulders that smelled of perfume, and

a long robe that showed off her breasts and hips. "How'd you get to know her?" he asked Lye.

"A friend of mine, a bookie, introduced us at the track," Lye said. The conversation made him uneasy; he felt his mouth beginning to tighten. "I drove her home that afternoon, and—" He shrugged. "Well, I started seeing her, that's all."

"You must have hidden talent," Amato said, staring deliberately and cruelly at Lye's twisted mouth. "You ain't the best-looking guy in the world, you know."

"I get along," Lye said, trying to control his growing tension.

"Maybe it's them prayers of yours being answered," Amato said. "You prayed when you were in jail, but God didn't get you out, Joe. I guess the prayers went into another account."

"How the hell would I know?" Lye said, lighting a cigarette and throwing the match aside nervously. "Things just work out, that's all."

"Then why pray?" Amato said.

"Why don't we talk about something else?" Lye said.

"Maybe you pray for the hell of it," Amato said. "For fun, maybe." He didn't know why he was needling Lye; it wasn't improving his own temper. "I can arrange for you to start praying again, if that's what you like. There's that Donaldson rap still hanging over your head. I guess you remember that."

Lye took a deep drag on his cigarette and tried to smile; but it was a ghastly effort. "Why should you send me back to jail?" he said. "I do my work. I'm with you all the way. You know that, Nick."

"Sure, I depend on you, Joe," Amato said, frowning faintly. "Let's forget it. How did Retnick sound?"

"No way in particular. He just said he'd come over."

"He may be your next job."

Lye nodded quickly. "I ain't worried." He felt the tensions easing in him, flowing mercifully from his rigid body. It filled him with shame to be so vulnerable to unreasoning fears; but those nights in the death cell had driven a shaft of terror into the deep and secret core of his manhood. The dream had come again last night, the violent red dream that repeated itself with the monotony of a stuck phonograph record. There were always the profane, laughing guards, the rush along the corridor, and then the rude altar and the straps that tightened across his bare chest until he could no longer breathe. And the guards stared at him, laughing obscenely, and there was nothing he could do about it. The dream sickened him; there were parts of it he had never been able to tell Kay about . . . .

Eleven

It was a few minutes past eleven when Retnick rang the bell at Amato's home. A cold wind hammered at the garbage cans set out along the curb, and street lights thrust cones of pale yellow light into the deep shadows along the sidewalk. Joe Lye opened the door, nodded jerkily at him, and said, "Come on along with me."

Retnick stepped past him and walked down a hallway to the kitchen. He wasn't worried about Lye's advantageous position behind him; it wasn't likely that Amato would try to kill him in his own home. Amato was sitting in his shirtsleeves at the kitchen table, smoking a short black cigar. The room was brightly lighted and smelled of peppers and ground coffee.

"What's on your mind?" Retnick said, as Lye drifted to one side of him and stood with his back to the wall.

Amato smiled and shook his fingers gently before his face. "You could turn that around, eh?" he said. "What's on *your* mind?"

"You wanted to see me," Retnick said. "Here I am."

"Come on, don't be so hard," Amato said. "How about some coffee?"

"Don't bother."

Amato shrugged and sighed. "So you're mad at me," he said. "Maybe you think you got reason to be. Maybe you think I put Hammy up to picking a scrap with you. Well, that's wrong, Steve. Hammy was working on his own, and I fired him for it. Now don't that prove I'm trying to get along with people?"

"Everyone knows you're a decent, generous guy," Retnick said, smiling coldly. "Tell me something new."

Amato cocked his head to one side and studied him for a second or two with narrowing eyes. Then he said gently, "There's no point being sarcastic. I'm trying to be fair. You thought I turned Hammy loose on you. All right, that's understandable. So you pick up my kid and rough him up a little. I don't like that, Steve. It was a dumb move. But I figure the two mistakes cross each other out. I'm ready to forget them. How about you?"

Retnick shrugged. "I've already forgot about the fight with Hammy," he said. "But he won't forget it that fast."

"Yeah, you really landed on him," Amato said slowly. "Now I got something else to say. How would you like his job?"

"Let's don't strain to be funny," Retnick said.

A little flush of color moved up in Amato's dark cheeks. "I ain't being funny, Steve. That ain't my way. The job pays two hundred bucks a week. And you can do better than that in a fairly short time. A business agent ain't a bad job, as I guess you know. You could make it in a couple of years if you played everything smart. You listening to me?"

"Sure, I'm listening," Retnick said.

"There's no point in worrying about the past," Amato said. "Here's how I feel. You live today. You got a living to make, a family to take care of, things like that. That you got to do *now*, today, not last year or five years ago. Carrying grudges don't pay no bills. So how about it? With a steady job you can get an apartment, get back with your wife, start living a good normal life again. And there's plenty of room with me, I guarantee you. So how about it?"

"I don't need a job," Retnick said slowly. Amato was serious, he knew, and that was the most disgusting part of it. Men compromised themselves in order to work. That was the rule and Amato understood it well. The choice was not between good or bad, but between bad and worse; a man was either an active participant in evil, or a silent accomplice. To stand in a middle ground meant economic suicide. And the necessity to compromise performed a moral alchemy on men; it altered them drastically and made them very easy to manage.

Amato shrugged and smiled. "Everybody needs a job, Steve."

"I'm wasting time. You have anything else to tell me?"

"Sure, sure," Amato said softly. He stood and came around the table, looking up at Retnick with cold sharp eyes. "You want to be a hard guy, eh? Make trouble, bother me. How long you think you'll last, eh?"

"What's your guess?"

"I don't have to guess," Amato said. Tilting his head to one side he flicked the back of his hand across Retnick's lapels in a contemptuous gesture. "Big tough guy, eh? Make trouble for me." Amato's grip on his temper was slipping; his voice was suddenly hoarse and thick. "Well, I tell you this. You're a big mouth, that's all. A big-mouth slob. I tell you now keep out of my way. You put your nose in my business and I'll cut it off for you. You forget about Ventra, forget about Ragoni, forget about my business. Then you'll stay alive. You bother me and you'll get your head blown off. You understand that?"

"Why should I forget about Ventra?" Retnick said, very softly.

"Because I say so," Amato shouted, and with the back of his hand slapped Retnick across the chest. "You do what you're told if you want to stay alive. I tell you—"

Retnick smiled and hit him in the stomach then, almost casually, and Amato bent over with a convulsive flurry of motion, hugging his arms tightly to his body and sputtering feebly through his straining mouth. His face was very red as he sagged helplessly against the kitchen table and put out one hand quickly to prevent himself from sliding to the floor.

Retnick turned with dangerous, menacing speed and struck Lye's forearm with a chopping blow of his hand. The gun Lye was raising clattered onto the floor, and he stiffened against the wall, one arm hanging uselessly at his side, his mouth twisting cruelly in his small pale face.

Retnick picked up the gun and put it in his pocket. He was breathing hard, trying to control his anger; it wasn't time to make a final move. Staring at Amato he said thickly, "You're lucky. Don't crowd it."

Amato's eyes were strange and wild. "You'll die for this, Retnick. I swear to God."

Retnick backed to the door, his hand sliding down onto the gun in his pocket. "Don't say anything else, Nick. I don't want to kill you."

Amato stared at him, breathing raggedly. He shook his head slowly from side to side then, knowing he was close to death.

"Not yet," Retnick said.

Outside he crossed the dark street and stopped in the shadow of a parked car. For a moment or so he watched Amato's door, but it remained closed; Lye wasn't coming after him tonight.

Retnick walked quickly toward the avenue. Turning left at the intersection he went by closed shops and markets, dark theaters that advertised Spanish subtitles. He wanted to find a phone, but everything was closed for the night. Two sailors across the street were arguing with drunken good humor about something or other, but there was no one else in sight. And there were no cabs. Retnick walked four blocks before coming on an all-night drugstore, and from there he put in a call to the Thirty-First. Lieutenant Neville was on another line, a clerk said. Would he hang on?

It was a short wait. Neville said hello, sounding tired and impatient.

"This is Steve," Retnick said. "I want to see you tonight."

Neville hesitated. Then he said, "Where are you?"

Retnick told him and Neville said, "This had better be

interesting. I was on my way home. I'll pick you up in ten minutes."

Retnick waited in the darkness a few doors from the drugstore, his back to a brick wall and a cigarette in his lips. When Neville's black sedan slowed down at the intersection, he moved out to the curb and held up his hand. The car pulled up alongside him and stopped. Retnick climbed in, Neville released the clutch, and they headed north on Tenth Avenue, cruising evenly to make the lights.

"Well, what is it?" Neville said.

Retnick glanced at him, and in the faint light from the dashboard he saw the hard lines around his mouth, the cold impersonal cast of his features.

"I've got a link between young Mario Amato and the guy who murdered Frank Ragoni," he said. "You want to hear about it?"

"I'm surprised you thought of me," Neville said dryly. "I got the impression earlier this evening that you figured me for one of Amato's boys."

"I didn't mean that," Retnick said. Neville's tone bothered him. Most of what he had learned about police work had come from Neville; not the routine of it, but the important intangibles, the need for patience and fairness, the objective, sympathetic consideration of human beings, this had come from Neville. There was no man in the department Retnick had respected more, no man whose approval meant more to him. But the significance and warmth of that relationship were gone. And it was he who had changed, not Neville. That was what seemed to hurt. "I need help," he said. He wished he could explain what he felt, but there was no way to unlock the words. "I've gone as far as I can on my own."

Neville slowed down and pulled over to the curb. When he cut off the motor the silence settled abruptly and heavily around them. There was very little traffic; an occasional truck rumbled past, briefly disturbing the silence. Ahead of them the wide avenue stretched into empty darkness. "Let me have a cigarette, Steve," Neville said. His voice was weary. Retnick gave him a cigarette, held a light for it, and then Neville pushed his hat back on his forehead and settled down in the seat. "You're going to tell me about Red Evans, I suppose," he said. "Is that it?"

"You know about him?" Retnick said. He couldn't keep the surprise from his voice.

"We try to earn our money," Neville said. "We know he drifted into Ragoni's gang, and disappeared the night Ragoni turned up missing. What have you got?"

"Quite a bit more," Retnick said. He told Neville what he had learned then; of Ragoni's letter to him in jail, of Ragoni's conviction that he knew who had killed Joe Ventra; of the winchman, Grady, who had been warned to stay off the job by young Mario Amato; of the accident by which Red Evans had almost killed Ragoni, and of Dixie Davis and his certainty that she was still seeing Red Evans in Trenton. "Here's how it looks to me," he said finally. "Ragoni was on the spot. Either because he knew who had killed Ventra, or because he was fighting as best he could to keep Amato and his hoodlums from taking over the local he belonged to. Mario Amato hired Red Evans to kill him and make it look like an accident. That didn't work, so Evans stuck a knife in him and blew. Doesn't that sound like the script to you?"

Neville shrugged lightly. "It could be, Steve."

"I talked to Mario tonight," Retnick went on. "He's a scared little punk. But he denied any connection with Evans. I could have beaten the truth out of him, but that wouldn't have held up in court."

"You're developing an odd common sense," Neville said, glancing at him sharply. "How did you get to talk to Mario?"

"I took him to my room."

Neville shook his head. "Steve, you're begging for trouble."

"Okay, okay," Retnick said. "But I'm getting what I want. I just left Nick Amato's home. Joe Lye called and asked me to come over, this was about an hour after I let

Mario go. Amato offered to forget the whole business, and then he offered me a job. When I told him what to do with it, he blew his top and told me to forget about Ventra and Ragoni. He threatened to kill me if I didn't. That caused a row. I belted Amato and slapped a gun out of Joe Lye's hand. Then I left. Don't you see this the way I do? If we throw young Mario and Red Evans together we'll get the whole story."

"And you want me to pick up Mario? Is that it?"

"Yes."

"I might," Neville said slowly. "I might if I caught him stabbing my wife or something like that."

"But not to sweat him?"

"This job isn't much, but it's all I've got," Neville said.

"So it's no, eh?" Retnick said, staring at him. "I give you a case against a murderer and you talk about losing your job. Is that it?"

"Now listen to me: you were trained as a cop and you know the meaning of evidence. But you seem to have forgotten it. You've got suspicions but you won't prove them by slapping people around. We've got two detectives working on the Ragoni murder. They'll stay on it until they get results. Leave the job to them. They're paid for it."

"I'm giving you a short cut," Retnick said. "But you want it the long way." He knew there was no point in further talk; no one cared as much as he did. No one had his reasons. Neville could wait for the slow turn of the wheel of justice, and meanwhile draw his pay and live his quiet pleasant life. But for him the waiting was over.

"Forget Mario Amato," Neville said. "We couldn't hold him for two hours. And what would I say when Amato sprung him? That I'd picked him up on the word of an ex-convict?"

"Supposing I got Red Evans?"

"We'll get Red Evans," Neville said. "You keep out of this. That's all I can give you, Steve, a piece of damn good advice."

"Save it," Retnick said. "Put it away with your pension."

"Okay, if that's the way you want it," Neville said angrily. "Where can I drop you?"

"The boarding house. It's on Fortieth and it's on your way. Otherwise, I wouldn't trouble you."

"You're a stubborn Polack," Neville said, and let out the clutch with an exasperated snap. The car leaped forward, the wheels whining at the pavement.

Retnick's street was dark and empty. The lieutenant coasted to a stop and let the motor idle. "Now hold it a second," he said, as Retnick opened the door. He turned toward him, a troubled frown on his face. "I want to say one more thing."

"More advice?"

Neville sighed. "I'm trying to help, Steve. In my way. I think it's the right way. But let's assume for argument's sake that I'm wrong. Say I'm a pension-happy cop who's afraid to rock the boat, afraid of hoodlums like Amato. Say that if you will. All I want you to do is think hard about what I've said. Get this chip off your shoulder and start thinking sensibly. Will you do me that favor?"

"I've thought about your advice," Retnick said. "Good night." Stepping from the car he slammed the door and went up the short flight of worn concrete steps to the doorway of his building. He took his keys from his pocket and turned halfway around to get some light from the street lamp. Neville started up the block under a rush of power, and Retnick turned back to the door and fitted his key in the lock. A high cold wind was blowing and a tin can tumbled along the gutter with a sudden clatter of sound. Retnick's key stuck and he pulled it out and turned once again to the light. And it was then that he saw the shadow of a crouching man moving along the line of cars at the curb. He hesitated an instant, feeling the sudden heavy strike of his heart, the warning tension in his muscles. The shadow moved again, rising slowly as the man came to a standing position behind a black sedan.

Retnick turned back to the door. Standing perfectly still

he counted to three, giving the man time to aim, and then he dropped to his knees and dove down the stairs toward the sidewalk. He landed on his right shoulder and tucked his head into his chest to keep from being brained on the concrete; the momentum of his lunge rolled him over, and he came to his feet in a crouch at the curb. And by then the street was echoing with a report of a gun and the scream of a ricocheting bullet. A second shot bounced from the front of the building, sending fine particles of brick whining into the darkness.

Retnick saw the flash of the gun's muzzle two car lengths ahead of him, on the curb side of the cars.

He held Lye's gun in his hand. The silence was complete now and he knew that Neville's car had stopped somewhere up the block. That meant the lieutenant had heard the shots.

The man who had fired at him was only two car lengths away, and Retnick heard the scuff of his shoes on the sidewalk as he moved closer through the darkness. There was no place for Retnick to hide. The cars were parked bumper-to-bumper along the curb and he couldn't slip between them to the street. He could only wait for Neville.

Somewhere down the block a window went up with a protesting shriek and a woman shouted into the silence. And the wind rattled the can near Retnick's hand.

He knew Neville would probably come back along the line of cars on the opposite side of the street. Crouching low he felt around for the tin can in the gutter. Then he tossed it over the cars into the street, and flattened himself on his stomach.

A big figure loomed in the darkness a dozen feet from him. Swearing hoarsely, the man clambered over the fenders of a car, and leaped into the street. He fired again, still cursing, and then Retnick heard Neville yell sharply, "This is the police. Drop that gun."

Retnick scrambled to his feet. A lamp on the opposite sidewalk threw a pale yellow light into the street, and Retnick saw a big man in a camel's hair coat, and saw the fear and rage working in his face as he wheeled and raised his gun in the direction of Neville's voice. A shot sounded off to the right and he heard the man cry out hoarsely. Turning in a frantic circle the man dropped his gun and hugged his stomach tightly with both hands. Finally he went down to his knees and began to sob. And when he fell forward his voice broke and he cried, "No!" in a high, incredulous voice.

Retnick put his gun away and climbed over the bumpers of a car to the street. Hammy lay sprawled on the pavement staring with wide frightened eyes at the dark sky, his big chest heaving for air. Noises sounded up and down the block as people shouted at each other from open windows. Several men were hurrying to the scene, their running footsteps loud and clear in the night.

Neville stepped from behind a car and crossed the street to Retnick's side. He was pale, and there was a sharp glint of excitement in his eyes. "Are you okay?" he said, watching Retnick closely.

"Yes. He missed twice."

Neville knelt beside Hammy. It was obvious the big man was dying. He looked lonely and scared and his face was very white.

"Did Amato tell you to get Retnick?" Neville said, speaking sharply and distinctly. "Come on, Hammy, get squared away before you die."

Hammy shook his head slowly. "I can't die," he said, wetting his lips. "It's not time. I'm young—" His voice broke and he began to cough.

"Who killed Ragoni?" Retnick said quietly.

Several men had crowded around them and Neville raised his head and glared at them. "Get back home where you belong," he said. "I'm a police officer."

The men backed off to the sidewalk and stared in fascination at Hammy.

"I don't know who killed anybody," Hammy said. He looked as if he were trying to cry. "You didn't have to shoot me, I had a lot ahead of me."

"Help us," Retnick said. Neville folded Hammy's fedora and slipped it under his head. "You don't owe Amato anything," Retnick said. "Who killed Joe Ventra? Do you know, Hammy?"

"Amato threw me out," Hammy said weakly. His eyes closed and he drew a deep breath. "Everybody said he killed Ventra. I don't know. Don't let me die."

"We'll do what we can, Hammy," Neville said. "Who says Amato killed Ventra? Tell us that." A police siren wailed in the distance. Neville shook Hammy's arm gently. "Tell us that," he said.

Hammy opened his eyes and reached for Neville's arm. "Wait," he said in a high clear voice. "It ain't over so soon. I just—" He tried to sit up then, staring in sudden fear and understanding at Retnick. When he began to cough the strength left his body and he slumped back to the pavement. Tears glistened in his staring eyes.

A squad car pulled up and a big partolman come toward them with a hand resting on the butt of his gun.

Neville got slowly to his feet and looked at Retnick. "You come on to the station with me," Neville said. "We'll need your statement. Then we'll have a talk."

Retnick gave his statement to a young detective named Myers, mentioning his fight with Hammy as a possible reason for the ambush. Neville typed out a report without bothering to take off his hat or coat. Then he tossed it in his basket and came into the file room and nodded at Retnick. "I'll wait for you on the sidewalk," he said.

When Retnick came out of the station Neville turned to him, his face sharp and white in the darkness. "Amato didn't wait long to take a crack at you," he said.

"He believes in direct action," Retnick said. "He doesn't wait for an airtight case. You could learn a lot from him."

"Let's stop yapping at each other," Neville said. "Do you know where Red Evans is now?"

"I think he's in Trenton."

"You said earlier that you could get him to New York. Does that still stand?"

"I don't need Red Evans," Retnick said coldly. "Didn't you hear Hammy say Amato killed Joe Ventra? That's all

I've been trying to find out."

"A hoodlum's word isn't enough to convict Amato."

"It's enough for me," Retnick said.

"Now listen," Neville said sharply. "We can get Amato my way. But you'll get nothing by acting like a one-man jury and firing squad. We need Red Evans, but we can't extradite him. If you get him, I'll pick up Mario Amato. Then we'll get the truth. And the truth will point at Amato."

Retnick hesitated a second, staring at Neville. "Do I have your word on that?"

"You have my word," Neville said. "But be careful, Steve. Red Evans is a very tough boy."

"Sure," Retnick said. "So was Hammy."

Twelve

From the Thirty-First Retnick walked to Tenth Avenue and picked up a cruising cab. What he had to do was simple and clear; find Red Evans and drag him to New York. How he would do this was neither simple nor clear, but he wasn't worrying about it. What worried him now was Davey Cardinal, and the thought of that hoodlum's interest in his wife. Retnick's concern was illogical, but he couldn't shake it. Why should he care what happened to her? The logical answer was that he didn't, but the logical answer wasn't accurate. He did care what happened to her and he didn't understand why. The driver looked around at him inquiringly, and Retnick gave him an address in the East Eighties, a half block from where he had lived with Marcia. Lighting a cigarette he tried to analyze his feelings on the ride uptown through the dark city. But he got nowhere. It was tied up with Amato, he decided at last. If Amato thought of hitting at him through Marcia, then that put her on his side, even though the involvement was needless and pointless. That must be it, he thought . . .

He paid off the driver and walked along the dark sidewalk, on the opposite side of the street from her apartment.

This was a neighborhood he knew well, although he had lived there only a few months. But in that time he had memorized the street; it was clearer in his mind than the streets of the lower east side where he had been born and raised.

Retnick stopped in the shadow of a tree and looked up at his wife's apartment. One light shed a faint golden glow through the curtains. She wouldn't be home yet, he knew. For a moment or so he stood completely motionless, staring at the windows of the apartment. It was difficult to realize that he had once lived there, and more difficult still to imagine what sort of man he had been then. The image of himself at peace, living normally and casually, was too strange and incongruous to believe in. He knew in an objective way he had once been happy, that he had laughed easily, that there had been friends in his life, and the warmth and sustenance of love, but when he tried to examine these memories they became distorted and blurred, twisting out of shape under the corrosive action of his anger.

But there were moments when he could think of Marcia apart from himself, without bitterness, without any feeling at all, as if she were some beautiful lifeless object he had known in a strange dream. It proved something to him that he could think of her at times without any sense of pain or loss. But what it proved he was never quite sure.

He always thought of her in motion; smiling or talking, looking up quickly to laugh at something in the paper, attacking the housework in brief shorts and sandals, her legs slim and brown and quick, fussing in the kitchen over dinner, making enough for six people because she was proud of his appetite. Her world was gay. And she had thought him too serious. "Don't *worry* so much," she used to say, laughing at him. But it wasn't worry that made him thoughtful, it was caution. Caution was in his background; it was part of the lower east side, part of working your way through school, part of being a cop. He wasn't afraid of life, but he had been taught to respect it. She could be careless and casual because she had never been hurt. This was a touching thing about her, the conviction that life was sunny and gay, that anyone you met could be your friend. He never quite understood this unreasoned optimism; it amused and puzzled him at the same time. But his attempt to fit her into any of the categories he knew had always failed; she was too direct in some ways, too subtle in others, and when he tried to hold her fast she went through his fingers like quicksilver.

He could think of her this way, dispassionately and calmly. It was the thought of her with someone else that brought up the cold lifeless anger, made his memories of her unendurable.

To his left the gleaming yellow light of a cab turned into the block. Retnick moved closer to the trunk of the tree as the cab slowed down and stopped a few doors from Marcia's apartment. A man climbed out, paid off the driver, and the cab started up again, picking up speed as it went by Retnick. The silence settled heavily as the noise of the motor faded away in the night. For a few seconds the street was quiet, and then Retnick heard the flat ring of the man's heels on the sidewalk. He came out of the darkness directly across from Retnick, and stopped to look casually at the doorway of Marcia's apartment. Then he strolled on, hands deep in his overcoat pockets, his hat brim pulled down low over his swarthy features. Retnick recognized him as he passed through the cone of light falling from the street lamp. Davey Cardinal, Amato's enforcer. Not a mad dog like Joe Lye, but a dangerous show-off, a man in love with his role as tough guy. Perfect for the job of terrorizing a girl.

Cardinal stopped two doors beyond Marcia's building, and glanced casually up and down the sidewalk. Then he stepped quickly into the shadows near the curb and merged with the darkness.

Retnick checked the gun he had taken from Joe Lye, made sure the safety chamber was off and that there was a round in the chamber. Then he crossed the street and walked down the sidewalk toward Cardinal, alert for any sudden movement in the shadows. When he saw the pale shine of his face, and the blur of his body beside a car, he stopped and said, "Hello, Davey."

Cardinal came out of the shadows slowly, a stocky man with a tight little grin on his dark features. He crossed a stretch of lawn to the sidewalk and looked up into Retnick's face. "You keep funny hours, Steve," he said.

"I thought you'd stopped siphoning gas out of parked cars," Retnick said. "I thought you'd turned into a big shot."

"I was obeying nature, that's all," Cardinal said. Still smiling, he touched Retnick's chest with the back of his hand. "But what I do ain't any of your business. And where and how I do it falls in the same class. Nothing about me concerns you, big boy. Keep that in mind. Keep that in mind while you turn your big tail and clear out of here."

"My wife lives just two doors from here," Retnick said gently. "She'll be coming home in a few minutes. Did you know that?"

Cardinal raised his eyebrows. "Maybe I'll run into her."

"No you won't," Retnick said, still speaking gently. Then he took the lapels of the little man's coat in one hand, and when Cardinal's arm dropped swiftly, Retnick drove the muzzle of his gun into his stomach with cruel force. A cry of pain broke past Cardinal's lips, and his hands came up from his pockets and tugged impotently at Retnick's wrist.

"Steve!" he cried out softly, as Retnick shoved him roughly against a tree. "You hurt me inside."

"Listen to me," Retnick said, staring into the pain and fear in his eyes. Their faces were inches apart and he could see the sweat on Cardinal's lip and forehead, the pinched lines of terror at the corners of his mouth.

"Steve—"

"Listen, I said. You beat it now. If anything happens to her, I'll come after you first. Understand that? I won't ask who did it, remember. I'll get you."

"Steve, I swear you got me wrong."

Retnick stared at him for another second or two in silence.

Cardinal wet his lips. "Don't kill me," he whispered. "God, don't kill me, Steve."

"I want to kill you," Retnick said. "I'd like an excuse. Remember that. Now get out of here."

Cardinal straightened his tie and without meeting Retnick's eyes slipped away from the tree and started up the sidewalk, walking like a man who is controlling a desperate impulse to break into a run.

Retnick watched the short dark figure until it disappeared in the shadows of the next block. He didn't think Cardinal would be back; the little hoodlum knew he wanted to kill him. Retnick drew a deep breath. It was stamped on him like a brand then, this need to hurt and destroy. Cardinal had seen it clearly.

A car door slammed behind him and Retnick turned quickly, irritated at himself for having failed to notice the sound of the motor. His wife said good night to the cab driver and started for the entrance of her building, pulling the collar of her coat up against the cold wind. Retnick stood perfectly still in the shadows, hoping she wouldn't see him. But she hesitated at the sidewalk and then turned uncertainly, seeming to sense his presence in the darkness.

"Steve?" she said softly. "Is that you, Steve?"

Retnick walked toward her, his hands in the pockets of his overcoat, and the cab driver, who had waited, said, "Everything okay, Miss Kelly?"

"Yes, Johnny, it's all right," she said, glancing at him with a quick little smile.

"Just checking," he said. "Good night now."

Retnick looked down at his wife and rubbed the back of his hand across his mouth. They were silent then in the cold darkness until the sound of the cab's motor had droned away in the next block.

Then she said, "The bartender told me you were at the club last night. Why didn't you wait?"

"I wanted a drink," he said. "Nothing else."

She shrugged lightly; her gray eyes were puzzled and hurt, but she managed a little smile. "And do you want a drink now? I have one upstairs."

"Never mind." It was hard to look at her, to see the tentative, hesitant appeal in her face. She had changed more than he had realized. Not physically; her skin and eyes, the clean grace of her forehead, these would never change. She would always be beautiful but she would never again be unafraid. The careless, unreasoned belief that everything would turn out for the best—that was gone.

"Why were you waiting here?" she said.

"It's too involved to go into," he said. "Look, could you

manage to get out of town for a week or two?"

"It's curious you should mention it. I'm planning to leave. Did you know that?"

He felt suddenly confused and angry. "How the hell would I know it? Where are you going?"

"Chicago. It's a better job, my agent thinks."

"You do what he says, eh? Just like that?" he said, snapping his fingers.

"Not quite. He's wanted me to leave for two years, but I thought there was something to wait for in New York."

"You'll be better off in Chicago."

"Why do you want me to leave?"

"I told you it's an involved business," he said. "I'm not making friends these days, and some of them might think of causing you trouble. It's a long shot, but it's there."

She was frowning slightly, watching him with thoughtful eyes. "And you'd care if something happened to me?"

There was no guile in her question; she seemed honestly puzzled by him now.

"I couldn't care less," he said, and his voice was bitter with anger at himself, at the stupidity of his answer. Why was he here if he didn't care? That's what she'd ask him next, trapping and hounding him with her eyes. "I don't want you dragged into this. I don't want you on my side, even by accident."

"Steve, Steve," she said, breathing the words softly. "Stop doing this thing to yourself." She caught his arm impulsively as he tried to turn away from her. "Look at me, Steve. Please! I want to talk to you, I want to tell you what happened—how it happened while you were away." She shook her head quickly, staring helplessly into his eyes. "It was so unimportant, Steve, so tragically unimportant. That's what I want to make you understand. It had nothing to do with my loving you. Can't you believe that?"

"I might," Retnick said, "if I were a complete fool. I suppose you told him I was unimportant—tragically unimportant in your nice phrase."

She took a step backward and withdrew her hand slowly from his arm. Then she said, "It's a waste of time to go on hurting me, Steve. If you knew me at all you'd realize you've hurt me enough." Her lips were trembling but her eyes were suddenly as cold as his own. "Maybe you think I should be stoned in the public square by the righteous daughters of the community? Or be beaten and branded and hung up by my thumbs? Is there any limit to what you think I deserve? How much should I pay for my mistake? I've been lonely and afraid for years. Isn't that payment of a kind? Isn't that enough? I'm in love with a man who can look at me as if I'm something loathsome. Isn't that some kind of payment? Well, to me it is. As far as I'm concerned the account is in balance. I've got nothing to be ashamed of. From now on I'll judge myself by my rules, yes, and by Father Bristow's. His rules are based on love, and yours are based on hate.'' She drew a deep, unsteady breath. "That's a long speech, but it's the last you'll hear from me."

"Wait a minute," he said.

"No." She shook her head quickly, speaking the one word with difficulty. Turning, she hurried toward the entrance of her apartment. He saw the gleam of her slim legs as she began to run, and he knew from the way she held her shoulders that she was weeping.

"I never wanted to hurt you," he shouted, but the door was already closing swiftly against his words.

Why had it happened to him? he thought, rubbing both hands over his face. He realized his mind was spinning senselessly, demanding answers to impossible questions. There was no reason to any of it; his life had been smashed casually and carelessly, destroyed in a whimsical collision with another's will. The only way to give it sense was to destroy whoever ordained these fateful collisions. An uncomfortable chill went through his body at the thought, and he shook himself quickly and began walking. He knew then that part of his hatred had shifted from Amato to someone infinitely more powerful. What worried him was that his anger was directed at someone he no longer believed in. It was this that made the shadows of the night, and the shadows in his mind, so strange and menacing.

Thirteen

Retnick lay on his bed smoking one cigarette after another, unable to find relief from his painful, turbulent thoughts. When a knock sounded on the door he got quickly to his feet, grateful for the distraction. Mrs. Cara stood in the hallway, an anxious and worried frown on her face.

"Mr. Retnick, I shouldn't bother you, but one of my old men is sick." She sighed and shook her head. "Not sick but drunk. He is weeping and drinking and I can't do nothing for him. I thought you could talk to him, maybe."

"What good would that do? If he wants to drink he'll drink."

"But he's not like that. Mr. Nelson is very steady all the time. Something just happened to him, that's all."

"You could call the cops," Retnick said.

"Oh, I wouldn't do that. He's a very nice man."

"Where is he?"

She smiled then, and some of the worry left her eyes. "Good, I show you. Come with me. Maybe another man can help him."

Mr. Nelson had a room on the first floor at the back of the house, a clean, neat cubicle with a window opening on an air shaft. He was lying on the bed staring at the ceiling, a tall thin man with silver-gray hair and gentle brown eyes that were sunk deep beneath bushy eyebrows. A half-empty bottle of whisky was on the floor near his trailing hand. He was fully dressed. His overcoat was folded over the back of a chair but he still wore a gray wool muffler. He had been crying, obviously; his nose was red and tears glittered in his staring eyes.

"You go back to bed," Retnick said to Mrs. Cara. "I'll sit here with him awhile."

"Can I get him anything?"

"I don't think so."

Nelson was apparently unconscious of their presence, but Retnick knew from the altered rhythm of his breathing that he had heard their voices. He pulled up the chair and sat beside the bed. Mrs. Cara looked uncertainly at the two men for a moment, and then sighed and tiptoed from the room.

"You can't help," Nelson said, without looking at Retnick. His voice was unexpectedly clear. "You might as well go, too. I'm not likely to become violent."

"You gave Mrs. Cara a scare."

"I didn't mean to. I—she's a good friend of mine. But I couldn't help it."

"She'll understand. She's just worried about you, that's all. You mind if I smoke a cigarette?"

"No, I don't mind. But you might as well go back and sleep. You can't help me."

"I'll just finish the cigarette then," Retnick said.

Nelson said nothing for three or four minutes. Retnick glanced around the small, tidy room; it was a still life of sterile loneliness. No snapshots, no pictures, no personal notes. The clutter of life was absent; the change and keys to use tomorrow, the stamped letter to mail on the way to work, there were no such things in this wrapped-up little box. A toothbrush stood in a clean glass on a shelf above the sink, and a bar of soap gleamed dully in the bright light. But they looked new and unused, like props in a department store window. Except for a tiny crucifix above the bed the walls were bare.

"My cousin died this morning," Nelson said, in his clear distinct voice. "That's—well, that's why I got drunk. Would you explain that to Mrs. Cara?"

"That's too bad," Retnick said. "She'll be sorry to hear it."

Nelson shook his head. "She didn't know him. I haven't seen him for fifteen years. He lived in Boise. He was a school teacher. Never married. But he was the only relative I had. It—just hit me today. I'm alone. There's nobody to bury me. The police will come when I die and they won't know what to do with my body. I—I just started drinking this morning. I couldn't stop thinking about what would happen to me, and I couldn't stop drinking. I'm not a drinking man. I worked thirty-two years in the post office and I don't suppose I had a dozen glasses of beer in all that time. You might as well go to bed, mister."

"When I finish the cigarette," Retnick said. His eyes moved to the crucifix, and he stared defiantly at the suspended figure. "You believe in God, don't you?" he said.

"I don't know. Not enough, maybe. I don't know."

"What did you do in your spare time when you were working?"

"I used to go out to the track," Nelson said. "I never bet, but I liked to watch horses. Thoroughbreds, I mean. I was born in Virginia and I got the look of them stamped in my head. I just like to watch them run." He smiled nervously and turned to look at Retnick. "You ever do that?"

"No, I was born on the east side. I thought horses came with milk wagons attached to them until I was about ten, I think."

"Well, you missed something. They're pretty to watch, I tell you."

"Maybe you could show me what to look for some day. They'll be running at Belmont in a few months."

"Sure they will. I'd be glad to show you, too. A kid misses a lot growing up in the city."

He was okay now, Retnick knew. Maybe he could even get to sleep. "How about a nightcap?" he said casually.

"You go ahead. I—I think I had enough."

Retnick rinsed the toothbrush glass, and poured himself a small drink. Then he said good night. But Nelson didn't answer him. His eyes were closed and his breathing had become regular.

When Retnick stepped into the dark hallway, Mrs. Cara put her head out of her door. "He's all right?" she asked him quietly.

"I think so. His cousin died this morning, and it hit him hard. But he'll be okay."

"I'm glad. He's a nice man. He's lived here eighteen years."

"Good night," Retnick said, but Mrs. Cara put her hand on his arm. "You were good to him. Your voice was almost like a woman's. You don't mind my saying this, I hope, but it ain't like the voice you used with your wife on the phone."

Retnick stared at her. "My trouble didn't come from a bottle. And it won't go away with a hangover."

"Things are never as bad as you think they are, Mr. Retnick. You remember that."

"Sometimes they're worse," Retnick said. "Good night."

He slept little that night and was up at six in the morning. He went to the corner restaurant for coffee and returned to his rooming house without bothering to eat breakfast. Today he had to look for Red Evans. This was Thursday, Dixie Davis' day off, and if she followed her customary pattern she would go to Trenton to meet Evans. Retnick decided to pick her up there. That would be less risky than attempting to trail her from New York.

The day was clear and crisp with an occasional flurry of snow in the air. Two men stood talking together in front of his rooming house. They were staring at the place in the street where Hammy had died. Retnick heard one of them say, "The guy who shot him was a cop. It says that in the paper. Some luck, eh? Pull something and find a cop in the same block waiting for you."

Retnick let himself into the room, trying not to think of anything at all, trying particularly not to think of his wife. That was over. She would go to Chicago and he would stay here with his dark heavy thoughts. The little cat, Silvy, blinked at him from an open drawer, stretching comfortably on his small stack of new shirts. He put her down on the floor and then took Joe Lye's gun from his pocket and looked at it for a moment, unable to decide whether or not to take it with him. There were risks either way. But he finally decided against it. He would go right back to jail if he were picked up carrying a gun. He put the gun under his shirts, closed the drawer and left.

It was an hour's ride to Trenton and by eight o'clock he had taken his post in the waiting room, sitting where he could watch the passengers who got off the New York trains. He spent the morning in the dusty, overheated room, using a newspaper to shield his face when people trickled in off the hourly trains. He wasted the morning and most of the afternoon before he became convinced that she wasn't going to show. It would have been more reasonable to trail her from New York and take the risk of being seen, he thought. Evans had probably left Trenton when he heard that Retnick was looking for him.

It was five o'clock when he got back to New York. He ate a sandwich and drank a cup of coffee, and then tried to find a cab. But the evening rush had started by then and the increasingly heavy snow had created traffic snarls throughout the midtown section. Retnick joined an exasperated group of people under a hotel canopy. A red-faced doorman stood in the street whistling for a cab with pointless optimism, while the snow fell softly and silently into the black congested city.

Retnick didn't get to Dixie Davis' apartment until almost seven o'clock. In the foyer he brushed the snow from his hat and shoulders before pressing her buzzer. She answered almost immediately, "Who is it?"

"Retnick," he said. "Remember?"

"Sure. What's on your mind?"

"I want to see you."

"Look, buster, there's a thing called a telephone," she said. "People use it to make dates with."

"I didn't have time to call," he said. "This is important."

There was a brief silence. Then she said, "Important to who? You or me?"

"It could be for both of us."

"Okay, come on up."

She was waiting for him in the doorway, a bored little smile twisting her freshly painted lips. Except for her eyes, which were cold little points under the red bangs, everything about her was designed as part of an obvious piece. The red silk dress straining tightly at the curves of her small body, the sheer nylons and wedge-soled ankle straps, the huge junk bracelet on her wrist, they all advertised an old, old product.

"Well, what's the good news?" she said. "You strike gold in a back tooth or something?"

"It's better than that," he said, smiling slightly. He strolled past her into the scrupulously neat and impersonal room. "We're all alone, eh?" he said, tossing his hat into a chair.

"Make yourself at home. You want a robe and slippers maybe?"

"It's a tempting idea."

"Okay, stop clowning," she said, staring at him coldly. "What's on your mind?"

"You don't sound very friendly," he said.

"I don't like guys barging up here like it was a saloon with a free lunch," she said. "I told you once, I'll tell you twice, use the damn telephone if you want to see me."

Retnick stared at her, his face and eyes hardening slowly. "I don't want to see you," he said. "Given a choice I'd prefer to play pinochle with somebody's eighty-year-old aunt. But I don't have a choice."

"You know where the door is," she said, putting her hands on her small, bony hips. "If you don't like it here, blow."

Retnick's smile did something ugly to his eyes. "You're pretty tough, aren't you?"

"I get by, buster. I take care of me and mine."

"But you're sitting in a very rough game," Retnick said. "You could get hurt. Doesn't that worry you?"

"I sleep just fine," she said.

"You're still seeing Red Evans," Retnick said slowly. "And he's a murderer. I didn't buy the cute story about the trusting little doll who lost her heart and bankroll to the con man. Life in Canada, a big fresh start, it was all corn, Dixie. Where is he? That's what I'm going to find out."

She laughed softly. "You're an ex-con who got kicked off the police force for murdering a man. Do you think that makes you something special? You think I'll get down on my knees for a creep like you? Get this straight now, buster: if I see Red Evans that's my business. He could be a murderer fifty times over and he'd still be a better man than you are."

Something in her manner puzzled him; she was relishing this moment, chin raised, eyes flashing, playing it as if she were facing an audience.

"You could get hurt in this deal," he said, watching her closely. "Hasn't that occurred to you?"

"I'm scared to death," she said.

Retnick caught her suddenly by the shoulders and jerked her close to him. "I'll bet you don't want to get hurt," he said softly.

The speed and power in his hands had wiped the wise little sneer from her face; she stared up at him, breathing unevenly, terrified by the strange look in his eyes.

"Don't," she whispered, and her eyes flicked past him to the closed bedroom door. It was an involuntary betrayal; she looked quickly back at Retnick, a new fear touching her face.

An audience, Retnick thought, and a little shock went through him. They weren't alone.

He heard the metallic whisper as the doorknob turned and he saw the straining effort Dixie was making to keep her eyes on his face. Raising his voice he said, "You said you'd finger him for a thousand bucks. So why stall? You want more dough?"

"Don't move," a voice behind him said quietly. "That's good. Now take your dirty hands off her. And don't turn around."

Retnick released the girl and she backed away from him,

grinning with relief. She rubbed her thin shoulders and said, "We'll see what a big man you are now, buster."

Fast expert hands went over Retnick's clothes and body. Then the voice said, "Okay, big shot, let's look at you."

As Retnick turned, a fist struck the side of his face and the sharp edge of a ring slashed across the cheek bone. The man who struck him stepped back quickly, the gun in his hand centered on Retnick's stomach. "All right, start something," he said, smiling faintly.

Retnick touched his cheek and felt the warm blood under his fingers. "You're Red Evans, eh?" he said.

"Yeah, that's it. How come everybody thinks you're dumb? You sound real sharp to me."

Evans was a tall man with sloping shoulders and a loose, reckless mouth. His hair was bright red, and he needed a shave; the lamplight glinted on the blond whiskers along his heavy jaw. He wore a gaily colored sports shirt with dark slacks, and his brown eyes looked muddy and dangerous.

"The love tap was necessary," he said, balancing himself on the balls of his feet and keeping a safe distance from Retnick. "My story goes like this: you broke in, started beating up my friend and I had to kill you in self-defense. Does it sound all right? You used to be a cop. You should be a good judge."

Retnick shrugged. "It sounds okay. But what's your story for Ragoni? Did you kill him in self-defense too?"

"I don't need any story for Ragoni," Evans said, and he wasn't smiling any more. "I never touched him. But it annoyed me when I heard you were talking pretty loud about me and Ragoni. That kind of talk can cause trouble. I checked with Amato and he told me you got this delusion I killed your pal. So I decided to come over and set you straight."

"You didn't trust Amato to handle it, eh?"

Evans said gently, "They sounded a little scared of you. Tough cop and all that crap. But things like that don't scare me, Retnick."

"Before you shoot you'd better be sure your little chum

here will back up the story."

Evans smiled at Dixie. "She'll back me up, she's smart."

"Sure, she's smart," Retnick said. "She offered to lead me to you for a thousand bucks."

Dixie laughed softly. "Did I, big shot? Did I lead you to him? Or was it the other way around?"

"She held out for more dough," Retnick said, watching Evans. He had little hope this would work. They weren't fools, they were shrewd and tough and ruthless.

"So she's double-crossing me," Evans said, with a sigh. He looked sadly at Dixie. "You're a naughty one, selling out the old redhead."

"It's funny," Retnick said, hardening his voice. "Real funny. Cops make most of their pinches because clowns like you have such fine senses of humor. How do you suppose I knew you killed Ragoni? You think I heard it on a newcast?"

Evans' expression changed slightly. He still smiled, but a wary glint appeared in his muddy eyes. "Okay, big shot, where'd you hear it?"

"Ask her," Retnick said.

"Sure," Evans said slowly. "I'll ask her. Dixie knows better than to kid around with me."

"He's just trying to steam you up, Red," Dixie said. One thin hand moved uneasily along the seam of her skirt. "I never told him anything."

"But he knows something," Evans said, looking thoughtfully at Retnick. "If he ain't guessing, then somebody's been talking."

"I'm guessing, sure," Retnick said. "I guess Mario Amato paid you to do the job on Ragoni. And I guess it was Mario who got you the job on the winch in Ragoni's crew. And I guess it was just damn carelessness when you almost hit him with a load of freight." He smiled coldly at Evans. "You want me to keep guessing?"

"You know about Mario Amato, eh?" Evans said. He looked genuinely puzzled. "Who's been talking to you?"

"Ask her," Retnick said.

Evans sighed deeply. "You goofed that time, big shot. I never told her about Mario."

"Somebody did," Retnick said. "Before you blast me and hit tomorrow's front pages, ask yourself who's been spreading the news about you."

"Red, wake up!" Dixie cried. "He's just stalling. Can't you see that?"

"Something cute is going on," Evans said. He looked mad and dangerous. "Come here, baby. Don't cross in front of him or you'll get a bullet through you."

"What do you want?"

"Just come here."

When she reached his side he put an arm around her and twisted his fingers into her hair. His eyes and gun stayed on Retnick. "I want to get things straight," he said, very quietly. "We'll take our time and find out what's going on. You first, Dixie," he said, and forced her head back until the tendons in her throat stood out tightly under the white skin.

"Red, don't!"

"I'm not going to hurt you," he said. "I just want you nice and quiet. Now listen: if you talked to anybody I got to know about it. Understand me? Maybe somebody put pressure on you or offered you a big payoff. That's okay. I don't care if you talked. But I got to know if I'm being fitted for a frame."

"Red, I swear to God," she cried.

"Let me finish. If you squealed say so. I won't hurt you. But I got to know."

"I swear I never talked, Red. Stop it, please."

"I think I believe you, baby," Evans said, watching Retnick with his muddy, dangerous eyes. "Now it's your turn, big shot. Where'd you get your information?"

Unconsciously, his hand tightened in Dixie's hair, and she said hoarsely, "For God's sake, Red, stop it!" The words were thick with pain in her straining throat, and tears started in her eyes. She tried to drive a sharply pointed heel into his foot, and then her right knee jerked upward in a spasmodic, convulsive reaction and knocked his gun hand into the air.

Retnick was on him like an animal. He caught Evans' up-raised wrist with one hand, his throat with the other, and slammed him backward across the room. The rush of his body knocked the girl spinning to the floor and sent a chair crashing crazily onto its side. Evans' body struck the wall with a crash, and Retnick saw the dazed pain and fear streak into his eyes when his head snapped against the wall.

"Drop the gun," he said, holding him by the arm and throat. "Drop it!"

Evans struggled against him, desperately trying to twist his pinioned hand and bring the gun to bear on Retnick.

"Tough guy," Retnick said, and closed his fingers with all his strength on Evans' wrist.

Evans screamed in pain, the sound of it high and incredu-lous in his throat, and the gun clattered from his distended fingers to the floor. Retnick hit him in the stomach then, and something brutal and guilty within him savored the impact of the blow and the explosive rush of air from Evans' lungs.

Breathing heavily, he stepped back and let him slide to the floor. He picked up the gun, dropped it in his pocket and stared for a second or so without feeling compassion at Evans' red, straining face and jackknifed body. Finally he looked at the girl who sat on the floor supporting her weight with one outstretched hand. Her eyes were wide with terror as she stared at him.

"Get up," he said.

"Don't hurt me, please."

"Get up. Keep quiet and you'll be okay."

Retnick walked to the phone and put in a call to the Thirty-First. Watching Evans, he told the clerk who an-swered to put him through to Lieutenant Neville. When Neville came on, Retnick said, "I got him. Evans. Can you pick him up right away?"

Neville whistled softly. "Is he marked up?"

"Nothing that will show."

"Where are you?"

Retnick told him and Neville said, "Sit tight."

Retnick put the phone down and lit a cigarette. Inhaling deeply, he felt some of the tension dissolving in his body. But he felt no elation or triumph. Only a curious bitterness and distaste.

"You're working with the cops?" Dixie asked him in a small, uneasy voice.

"That's right."

"You made him think I crossed him," she said. Staring at Evans a little shudder went through her body. "What'll happen to me when he gets loose?"

"Maybe he won't get loose."

"But if he does?"

"That's your problem."

"What have you got against me?"

"Nothing," Retnick said shortly.

She was very pale and her lips were trembling. "Why did you put me in this spot?"

"You put yourself in it," Retnick said, staring at her. "This guy is a killer. He killed a man he'd never seen before, slipped a knife between his ribs for a piece of change. And you knew about it. You thought he was a hero." Retnick made an abrupt, angry gesture with his hand. "Behind every one of these vermin is a dummy like you, loving them, protecting them, treating them like glamour boys. Until you get in the middle. Then you get religion. You think that—" Retnick stopped and ground out his cigarette. He felt disgusted with himself. "You'll be okay," he said.

She was weeping now. Fear had stripped the cynical, wise-guy mask from her face. She looked suddenly childish and vulnerable. Even the cheaply sexy clothes seemed incongruous on her small thin body, like props borrowed from an older sister.

"You don't know him," she said. "You don't know what he's like when he's mad."

"He'll have enough problems without worrying about you."

The buzzer sounded and he went to the speaking tube that was hooked to the wall. He made sure it was Neville, then pressed the button that unlocked the inner door of the foyer.

Neville and Kleyburg walked into the room a few seconds later. Kleyburg put a hand on Retnick's arm, his eyes going worriedly to the blood on his face. "You okay, Steve?" he said.

"It's nothing serious."

Neville was staring down at Evans. "They never look worth the trouble they make," he said. Then he nodded at Dixie, his pale face completely without expression. "Who's this?"

"The girl friend," Retnick said.

"You've got to protect me," Dixie said, smiling nervously at Neville.

"Will you testify against him?" he said.

"There—there's nothing I could tell you," she said, as her eyes slipped away from his contempt. He turned to Retnick, dismissing her completely. "Did you get anything from him?"

"He's your boy," Retnick said. He was sure Evans was listening, so he said, "He knows Amato is trying to frame him and keep the kid in the clear."

Neville picked up the cue. "Amato will get away with it too."

Evans straightened himself painfully to a sitting position. "You guys are real comedians," he said. "Comic book cops, that's what you are."

Kleyburg looked at him with a pleased smile. "On your feet, buddy. We're going to take you some place where you can tell us your life story. I'll bet it's good."

Neville touched Retnick's arm and drew him aside. "You fade," he said quietly. "We'll pick up Mario Amato now and toss these two babies together. I'll call you when there's a break."

Fourteen

Retnick waited in his room for Neville's call. He sat on the edge of the bed smoking one cigarette after another and checking his watch every few minutes. It was after midnight now; five hours had passed since Evans and Mario had been arrested.

The lamp on the bureau cast a pale yellow light over the old furniture, the dusty, rose-patterned furniture, and drew dark lines across Retnick's rock-hard face. Nothing could slip, he was thinking. Evans was in a savage, nervous mood, half-convinced he was being measured for a frame. Young Mario was a weakling and a fool. Slam them together and you'd get an explosion of squeals and denials. But it hadn't happened yet.

He tried to picture what was going on at the Thirty-First, knowing the cat-and-mouse game Neville would play, knowing the mood of casual but ominous tension he would generate for the benefit of Evans and Mario Amato. He had been part of that scene himself dozens of times but tonight it was difficult to bring it into clear and vivid focus. Another idea slipped softly into his mind, threading itself like elusive music into his hard and bitter thoughts. Tonight would dissolve the swollen fury he had lived with for five years, and then he could see his wife again. Maybe he would understand her then.

The phone rang shrilly and before the echoes died away

Retnick was through the door and into the wide dark hallway. He lifted the receiver and said, "Yes?"

"Steve?" It was Neville's voice, edged with weariness.

"Yes. Did they crack?"

Neville drew a deep breath. "It's a bust, Steve. They aren't talking."

"They will, they've got to," Retnick said, tightening his grip on the receiver.

"We used all the tricks, Steve. Nothing worked."

"Evans practically admitted to me that he killed Ragoni," Retnick said angrily. "And he practically admitted that young Mario Amato paid him to do it."

"They won't admit anything now," Neville said. "Now listen: we picked up Mario at his uncle's house four or five hours ago. Kleyburg made the pinch. Amato raised hell. He told his nephew he'd have him out by morning. Mario believed him, I guess. He won't talk. And neither will Evans. I've had two calls from downtown. They're getting hotter about this pinch all the time. So far they buy my story. But I can't convince them much longer."

"So you'll turn them loose," Retnick said bitterly.

"I'll have to. I expect Amato here in an hour or so with a writ for Mario. After Mario walks out Evans will know damn well we were bluffing. I could hold him for a while but what's the point? He isn't going to talk."

Retnick stared down the dark hallway. He could see the yellow gleam of a street lamp through the glass doorway. He said quietly, "Look, lieutenant, is that creep Connors around? You know, the detective on Amato's string."

"Sure he's around. He's trying to find out what's up. But I've kept him away from this deal. Why?"

"Tell him young Mario has spilled everything," Retnick said.

Neville was silent a moment. Then he said wearily, "Steve, you're out of your mind. Connors would pass that to Amato. Do want to back a hunch against that boy's life?"

"I'm not interested in Mario's life," Retnick said. "I want to hang Amato. If he thinks his nephew has squealed on him he'll play into your hands."

"No!" Neville said, snapping the single word out with explosive force. "I've gone as far as I can with you. I'm not going to set up a murder to prove that your guess is right. Damn it, Steve, think! Do you realize what you're asking?"

"It was just a thought," Retnick said. He'd been foolish to hope for Neville's help on a shady maneuver; Neville played to strict rules. "I guess we struck out," he said.

"Don't worry, we won't stop here," Neville said.

"Sure," Retnick said. Then he said casually, "Is Kleyburg around, by the way?"

"No, I sent him home an hour ago. Why?"

"It wasn't important. It will keep."

"Get some rest, Steve. And don't think we're licked."

"Of course not. Thanks for the try, lieutenant."

When Retnick replaced the phone he stood for a moment in the darkness, a strange little smile touching his lips. Neville wouldn't help him. But Kleyburg would.

The old man was obviously ready for bed; he wore a dark-blue flannel robe with slippers and the ends of his gray hair were still damp from a shower. He peered up at Retnick, who stood in the shadows of the doorway, and a surprised smile touched his face. "Steve, this is wonderful," he said. "I couldn't imagine who it was at this time of night."

"I know it's late."

"Forget it. Come on in."

"Thanks." Retnick walked into the warm, comfortable room and dropped his hat on a sofa. Kleyburg had been reading; there was a cup of coffee on the table beside his chair, and a sports magazine on the ottoman. The air smelled pleasantly of coffee and pipe smoke.

"How about a drink, Steve? I'm a long way from turning in. We can jaw away all night if you like."

Retnick looked steadily at him. "Evans didn't talk. Neither did young Mario. That's why I'm here. I need help."

"Sure, Steve. What do you want?"

"We've got to make Evans talk."

Kleyburg spread his hands helplessly. "Easier said than

done, Steve. We've tried everything. On him and young
Mario. But they didn't break. They're more scared of Amato
than they are of cops."

"There's one thing you can try, Miles."

"Yeah? What's that?"

"Tell Amato his nephew squealed."

Kleyburg smiled uncertainly as the silence stretched and
grew in the small, comfortable room. "Now, Steve," he
said at last, still smiling nervously and uncertainly. "Amato
wouldn't believe us. He'd know we were bluffing."

"Not if he got the word from Connors," Retnick said.

Kleyburg's smile faded slowly. He gestured nervously
with one hand and then, to gain time it seemed, removed
his glasses and began to polish them with a handkerchief
he took from the pocket of his robe. "Yes, he'd believe
Connors," he said finally. "That's what he pays him for.
Information. But what good would that do?"

"The word would get back to Evans," Retnick said. "Right
now he's ready to blow sky high. If he thought the kid had
talked he'd start singing, too. And he'd tell us who paid
him to kill Ragoni."

Kleyburg shook his head quickly and turned away from
Retnick. Without glasses he look weary and vulnerable; his
eyes blinked against the light and a tense frown gathered
on his forehead. "You—you can't be serious," he said.

"All it will take is one phone call. From you to Connors."

"No!" Kleyburg said, still shaking his head. "Good Lord,
Steve, do you realize what you're asking? Spreading the
word that Mario squealed would be like handing him a death
sentence. And that's a verdict only a judge and jury are
qualified to make. You know that, Steve. I'm a police officer, not an executioner."

"Nothing's going to happen to the kid," Retnick said.
"Amato won't kill his own nephew. All this will do is put
pressure on Evans. One phone call from you to Connors
can break Nick Amato. What are you stalling for?"

"Steve, don't ask me to do this," Kleyburg said, rubbing
a hand helplessly over his forehead. Turning away from

Retnick he looked at the picture of his sons on the mantel, staring at them as if he could find some strength and resolution in their earnest young faces. "I've never pulled anything shady or crooked in all my years on the force," he said, and it seemed as if he were speaking to his boys now instead of Retnick. "Maybe that's no claim to fame. But I slept nights. I never had any trouble looking at myself in a mirror." Sighing, he turned and looked up into Retnick's eyes. "You see why it's impossible, Steve? You're taking a chance on that boy's life. I can't go that far."

"You've got a fine bleeding heart for hoodlums all of a sudden," Retnick said bitterly. "I'm after the guy who framed me into jail for five years. But you won't lift a finger to help. All you'll do is make pious speeches about how honest you are and what a pity it would be if a pampered little creep like Mario got hurt. Did you forget that I got hurt too? I lost every goddamn thing that made sense in my life, but that doesn't mean anything to you. To hell with Retnick. This is Be-kind-to-the-Amatos week."

"Steve, don't talk that way," Kleyburg said. He rubbed his mouth nervously and glanced around the room, avoiding Retnick's eyes. "If—if you'd calm down you'd see I'm right about this."

Retnick walked to the mantel and picked up a picture of Kleyburg's older son. He stared at the grave young face, and a bitter smile touched his lips. Then he looked at Kleyburg. "How do you think you lived long enough to raise these kids?" he said quietly. "When we worked together who kicked open the doors, and walked into dark alleys? You or me?"

"Steve, I know you carried me, I know—"

"Sure, I carried you," Retnick said harshly. "I took the tough jobs and let you sit on your can in the car. You think I liked that? You think I was tired of living and wanted some hopped-up punk to blow my brains out?"

"Steve," Kleyburg said helplessly, but Retnick cut him off with an angry gesture. "You made your speech, let me make mine. I carried you because you had kids. Because they needed you alive and on a payroll. Otherwise they might have been on the streets. Think about that when you're sitting around in Florida on your pension."

Retnick put the picture back on the mantel and turned to the door. Kleyburg hurried after him and caught his arm. "Steve, wait a minute," he said, in a soft, pleading voice. "Don't leave this way. We were friends, remember."

With a hand on the door Retnick turned and stared at him. "Sure, I remember," he said. "You're the one who forgot it."

"Wait, please." Kleyburg rubbed his forehead and shook his head. He looked very tired and beaten; his lips were trembling and his eyes were dull and hopeless. "I can't let you go this way," he said, barely whispering the words. "I—I'll get the word to Connors."

Retnick caught his shoulders in his big hands. ''He's at the Thirty-First now. If he's gone try his home. And for God's sake don't be so obvious about it.''

"I'll handle it," Kleyburg said wearily. "We're working on a case. I'll call him about that and let him pump me. He thinks I'm an old fool anyway."

"That should work," Retnick said. "Don't worry about the kid. It's Nick Amato who's going on the hook."

Kleyburg nodded but his eyes slipped away from Retnick's. "I—I'm glad to be able to help, Steve. I know you carried me. Even if it was just because of the kids I appreciate it."

"We'll have a drink the day they hang Amato," Retnick said. "Make that call now."

Fifteen

It was an hour before dawn when Nick Amato walked into
the brightly lighted hallway of the Thirty-First precinct.
With him was an attorney named Coyne and a stockily built
man who wore a tweed overcoat and a checked cap pulled
down over his left ear. This man had several names which
were familiar to the police, but he was called Kerry along
the waterfront, in recognition of his tweeds and brogue and
his incessant, lively chatter about stake racing in Ireland.
He had been born on Pell Street in lower Manhattan and
had seldom been more than fifty miles away from the place
of his birth.

Amato stopped at the information counter and smiled apologetically at the gray-haired lieutenant on duty. A casual
observer might have guessed that his awkward little smile
was a kind of peasant's armor against the awe-inspiring
figure of the officer on duty. But the lieutenant was no
casual observer; he knew all about Amato's smile. Leaning
forward he said earnestly, "To speak plain, Nick, I thought
it was a damn shame to arrest your boy."

"Sure," Amato said, rubbing a finger along his nose. "It
scared the old woman half to death. Great police work.
Let's have him now. The lawyer, he's got the papers."

"A damn shame," the lieutenant said again as he accepted
the writ from the attorney. Raising his voice he yelled:

"Turnkey! Bring Mario Amato out here."

When Mario appeared he was smiling with a new strength and confidence. The eight hours in jail hadn't marked him physically; he didn't even look in need of sleep. What sustained him was the realization that he had handled himself damn well. He knew that. Joe Lye, Kerry, they couldn't have done better. For a while he had been so scared that he was damn near sick right in the lieutenant's office. Neville, that was his name, had all the facts, and seemed to regard Mario's confirmation of them as an irrelevant detail. A shrewd tough man! Mario would remember the contempt in his eyes for a long time. But it was over now, and he hadn't given them a thing.

"How come the delay?" he said to his uncle, very pleased to be able to joke about it. "These places ain't rest homes exactly."

"Things take time," Amato said. "The lieutenant's got your watch and wallet. Sign out and let's go."

Mario took his wallet from the lieutenant and put it in his pocket without counting the money. This struck him as a nice touch, a patronizing way of letting the cops know he thought they were too dumb to be thieves.

Amato smiled at him but the lights in his eyes were like the points of daggers. I was good to him, he thought. Cars, clothes, money, dames. Anna's little man, pink-cheeked, wavy-haired, with hands that had never known a day's work. My nephew, he was thinking, who would be watching goats on a rocky farm in Calabria if it wasn't for me. I made him a big shot. Just because he hangs his hat in my house and can tell people I'm his uncle he's a big shot. And he'd squealed. At the first hint of pressure he'd crumbled like a piece of stale cake.

Amato kept his little smile in place with a conscious physical effort. He had received Connors' call an hour ago, and since then his anger had been growing dangerously. Connors wasn't sure what the kid had spilled, but he said Neville was happy about it. So this wasn't over yet. They'd pick him up again and again, knowing he was soft and frightened, and eventually they'd get the whole story. If they didn't have it already . . .

Amato rubbed his damp forehead. Take it nice and quiet, he thought. But that was like telling a man with a ticking bomb under his bed to close his eyes and go to sleep. Amato's anger was streaked with a lugubrious self-pity; he felt surrounded by fools and ingrates. Hammy, who'd got himself killed in a stupid move against Retnick; and Joe Lye! Where in hell was Joe Lye? Amato had tried to find him after he'd got Connors' call, but with no luck. So he had been forced to use Kerry, who had a bad habit of boozing and talking too much.

"Let's go," he said to his nephew, and walked outside, making no attempt to conceal his disgust. Kerry joined him on the sidewalk. "Should I be on my way?" he asked briskly.

"Yeah, get going," Amato said, without looking at him. "Don't mess this up. Evans says she's the one who fingered him. All he wants is to pay her off." Amato shook his head and frowned into the darkness. "You guys got to have dames. And you got to tell 'em everything. Brag about every job you pull. Then the cops get hold of them and you act surprised because they squeal. It's the way all you dopes get in trouble."

Kerry smiled faintly. "Sure and that will never change, Nick. I'll see you later." As Mario came out of the station Kerry turned and walked up the block, his leather heels ringing in the silence. He was whistling an Irish air and the melody was clear and sad in the cold, windy night.

Amato glanced at his nephew. "Was it rough?" he said.

"Hell, I could do it standing on my head," Mario said, grinning.

"You go home now. I want you to wait for me in your bedroom. You understand?"

"Look, Nick, I'm all right. I ain't even tired."

"Listen to me," Amato said. "As a favor, okay?"

Amato's attitude confused Mario. "Sure," he said.

"Go home. Wait for me in your bedroom. I'll see you in an hour. We'll have a talk about tonight."

"All right, Nick."

The attorney stood beside Amato and the two men watched Mario walk away toward the avenue. In spite of his uncle's disconcerting manner there was a new confidence in the lift of his head.

Coyne, the attorney, said, "What was this all about, Nick?"

Amato shrugged. "Cops killing time, I guess."

"I suppose. Can I drop you somewhere?"

"No, I got my car."

"Well, good night then."

Without answering him Amato turned and walked down the block to his car. He needed Lye now, and he thought he knew where to find him . . .

Kay Johnson lived in a tall and imposingly respectable apartment house on the east side. The street was quiet and empty and Amato found a parking place without difficulty. He knocked on the door of the building and peered through the wide glass frames for a sign of life in the lobby. This was great, he thought, savoring the sensuous rush of anger that ran through him. Nick Amato standing in the cold, waiting on Joe Lye's pleasure.

At the far end of the lobby elevator doors opened and a uniformed attendant hurried toward him fumbling with a ring of keys. The man peered through the glass at Amato, frowned indecisively, and then opened the door an inch.

"Kay Johnson," Amato said. "What's her apartment?"

"Six A, sir. But you'll have to phone from the lobby. Most of the tenants insist . . ."

"Okay, okay, we'll phone her," Amato said. "We disturb something, we disturb something. Is that character with the funny lip up there?"

"I wouldn't know, sir." The man led him to a carpeted alcove off the lobby, and nodded to a phone on a desk. His manner was cold and reproving.

I'll show them what crude is, Amato thought bitterly. East side snobs and Joe Lye playing the gent with Martinis and steaks. No place for Nick Amato. He was just good enough to pick up the checks . . .

Lye answered his ring in a sleepy voice. "Yeah?"

"This is Nick," Amato said good-humoredly. "I tried you earlier but you wasn't in."

"We took in a show and then hit a few spots," Lye said. "Was it something important?"

"So-so. I want to see you now. I'm downstairs."

"Downstairs?" Lye's voice shook slightly. "You mean in the lobby?"

"I guess that's the name for it. Can I come up?"

"Why—" There was silence on the line.

Asking permission, Amato thought. Explaining to her, while he covered the receiver with his hand. *I'll get rid of him fast, baby. You keep out of sight. I'll tell him you've got a headache.*

"Sure, Nick, come on up. 6 A."

"Thanks."

Lye met him at the door wearing a gaudy silk dressing gown over a white-on-white shirt and black trousers. He looked as if he had thrown his clothes on in a hurry; the robe was unbelted and a few strands of glossy black hair were plastered against his pale forehead.

"Well, come in, Nick," he said, trying to learn something from his face.

"Sorry to bother you this time of night," Amato said gently. "But I got a job for you."

"Yeah? Who is it?"

Amato didn't answer him. He was staring about the room, a pleased little smile on his lips. It wasn't as grand as he'd thought it would be and for some reason this made him feel better. He noted the record player and bar, the brilliant drapes and bright meaningless pictures, and continued to smile and nod with diffident approval.

"Very cute," he said. "Where's the girl friend? Headache?"

"No, she's just getting fixed up. Were you serious about a job?"

Amato stared at him. "Get out of that clown suit and into

your clothes," he said. "There's a job. You want me to do all the work while you lay around here and play footsie?"

Lye rubbed his thin hands together and they made a sound like dry paper rustling in the silence. "Stop riding me," he said, the words coming out in painful jerks. "If you ain't satisfied with me maybe you should get somebody else."

"Sure," Amato said slowly. "And then I'll send you back to catch up on your prayers. Back where you get in a full quota of Hail Marys every night."

A door opened behind him and he turned awkwardly and removed his hat. Kay Johnson smiled at him as she came into the room, her manner that of a flustered wife meeting her husband's boss under less than perfect circumstances.

"This is a wonderful surprise, Mr. Amato," she said. Smiling into his little brown eyes she knew with her sense of audience that she wouldn't fool him for an instant. Words and smiles would be useless against Nick Amato. She recognized his seeming diffidence for what it was, a front for a cynical and contemptuous estimate of people. And she realized also that her own act wasn't a very good one. All of her guile couldn't hide the fear in her eyes. The fear had been part of her so long that she had stopped trying to manage or conceal it.

"This is a nice place, Miss Johnson," Amato said. "If I'd known it was this nice I'd have stopped by sooner. If Joe asked me, that is."

"We've planned to have you up a half-dozen times," she said. "Now, wouldn't you both like a drink? Or coffee perhaps?"

"Take care of Nick," Lye said. "I'll get dressed."

"Are you going out?" She was out of character now; there was no pretty surprise in her manner, and her voice was dull with fear.

Lye walked rapidly into the bedroom and Amato said, "I'm sorry to break up the party, Miss Johnson."

"I suppose it's important," she said, staring at the bedroom door.

"In our business we work around the clock." Watching

her, he wondered if she really loved Joe Lye. It didn't figure. She probably was after his cash. That was why she put up with his cheapness, his twisted ruined face. And Lye was getting a bargain, Amato thought, as a strangely complex desire for her began to grow in him. Part of it was physical but there was something else, too. She was class. He had never had a woman like this, and he wondered why. Was it a guilty hangover from his stern childhood training, or was there some lack in him he hadn't recognized or admitted?

He saw with sharp irritation that she wasn't paying any attention to him at all. She paced restlessly, a tense expression around her eyes, and when he turned he saw the gleam of her slim white ankles and the soft press of her thighs against the silken robe. Did he want her because she was blonde and elegant? Because his people were peasants who would have bowed and tugged the peaks of their caps at a woman like this?

"I saw you in the movies once," he said. "That was quite a while back."

"I'm sure it was," she said.

"You played a college girl who didn't wear any make-up," he said, enjoying her strained smile.

"Yes, that was 'Ladies of the Chorus,' " she said.

"You should know. The guy you liked couldn't see you for dust, so you got a job in a cabaret. Then when you were all dolled up he fell in love with you without knowing you were the girl he knew in college."

She laughed and picked up a cigarette from the table. "I'm afraid it sounds just as idiotic now as it did then."

"The guy had a good reason to fall for you," Amato said, watching her. "You were clean and damned good-looking. What else does a man want?"

She saw that he wasn't going to light her cigarette so she did it herself and dropped the match into an ashtray. "I think you're drawing me out now," she said. "You want to hear me say something silly and female."

The door opened then and Lye walked into the room pulling up the knot in his tie. He glanced at Kay and said, "I left the radio on. How about going in and turning it off?"

"Of course," she said quickly.

When she had entered the bedroom Lye rubbed his hands along the sides of his trousers. He looked as if his nerves were stretched to the breaking point. "Okay, what is it?" he said.

"The kid," Amato said quietly.

"You're kidding!" Lye said, and his lips began to strain in spasmodic little jerks.

"I didn't come here to make jokes," Amato said. "He talked. He'll talk again." His voice was suddenly as sharp as a knife blade. "He's home now. In his bedroom. Anna goes to six o'clock Mass. You got to make it look a suicide."

"Nick, this is rough. Can't you figure out something else?"

"You don't like it?"

"No," Lye said.

Amato felt his anger swelling like a cancerous growth inside him. Nobody could take orders any more. That's why there was trouble on the docks. "Maybe you want to go back to jail?" he said in a low, trembling voice.

Lye turned away from him abruptly. The dream flooded his mind at Amato's words, everything in red, the guards, the altar, and in the middle of it his own soft, helpless body, waiting for the impersonal horror of the straps. "I—I just said we might figure out something else," he said.

"*We* don't figure things, *I* figure them," Amato said.

"Sure, sure," Lye said, speaking with difficulty against the constricting pressure around his chest. "I'm ready. Let's go."

Kay returned to the room then, and one hand went to her throat as she saw the tight, unnatural smile on Lye's lips. "What's wrong?" she asked anxiously.

"Nothing," he said, turning away from her. "Come on, Nick, let's go."

Amato smiled at him. "You go on, Joe. I'll take up that drink offer if it's still open."

"You're staying here?" Lye said dully.

"If it's all right with Miss Johnson," Amato said.

"Of course it is," she said.

"I'll check with you later," Lye said, looking at Amato. He hesitated, obviously reluctant to leave.

"It's late, Joe," Amato said gently.

Lye picked up his black overcoat from a chair, nodded jerkily at them and walked out the door. Amato was silent, smiling faintly, as he heard the faint whine of the descending elevator.

"What would you like to drink?" she asked him.

"Never mind." He dismissed the offer with a wave of his hand. "It's morning. No time to be drinking."

"I'm glad you stayed," she said. "I've wanted to talk to you for some time now."

He looked at her in surprise. "What do you want to talk to me about?"

She smiled nervously and lit another cigarette. "Joe would be furious with me for this," she said. "I may be wrong—" She drew a deep breath and tried to meet his eyes directly. "Why do you nag him about the time he spent in jail? Don't you realize how it upsets him?"

"It bothers him, eh?" Amato said slowly.

"You must realize that it does," she said. "I know it's a joke, a form of masculine humor that I don't understand perhaps, but it upsets him terribly. I'm sure you don't mean it seriously, but that needling about the death cell and his prayers, it's on his mind night and day."

"It's no joke," Amato said, smiling. "I'm looking for information. What was he praying for? That's all I want to know."

"If you won't be serious there's no point in discussing it."

"Oh, I'm serious," Amato said. He smiled at her but his eyes were narrowed and cold. "Maybe you can tell me what he's praying to? You know him pretty well. How come he prays when he's ready to die? To what does he pray? To who?" He swept an arm around the room, flushing with a sudden anger. "You think those are funny questions? Well, I'll tell you. You like dough, eh? You give me some sensible answers to them questions and I'll load you down with more dough than you ever seen in one lump before. If there's a God, then the prayers make sense. Ain't that right? But if there isn't a God, what's the sense of praying?" Amato turned away from her and shook his head irritably. For a moment he was silent, staring at the floor. "It's no time to be talking about it," he said.

"We never settle arguments about religion and politics, do we?"

"I wasn't talking about religion. I was talking about God."

She knew he was serious but his fears struck her as irrelevant and slightly comical; there were so many things to fear in life that she hadn't found time to fear God.

"How come you got mixed up with Joe?" he asked her bluntly.

"That isn't a very graceful way to put it, Mr. Amato."

"You need him, I guess. How long would you last without his dough?"

"With excellent managing, about three months."

He grinned at her. "And then what? Back to the movies?"

"Naturally," she said. "Or television or the theater. It would be simply a matter of picking or choosing." Her voice broke and she turned away from him quickly. "My agent still sends me Christmas cards," she said. "Isn't that an encouraging sign?"

"I could do more for you than Joe," he said. "You're no kid. You need things solid and secure. Joe Lye is one of six hundred guys who do what I tell him. He's nothing." As her expression remained unchanged he made an impatient gesture with his hand. "Well, how about it?"

She managed a smile and said, "I think it's dear of you to flatter me this way." This was safe ground. She had been maneuvering with middle-aged men for twenty years, and she could handle them with ease. It was a simple problem, unrelated to her fear of hunger and age, her terror of Joe Lye's nightmares and the small black gun he carried in his pocket. "I'll make you that drink now," she said.

"I want a yes or no," he said stubbornly.

"Very well," she said. "Before anything else I want to be your friend. Do you understand what I mean?" This was a tested armor, she knew, short, ambiguous questions put very earnestly and thoughtfully.

"Forget the drink," Amato said dryly. He knew she was telling him no, tactfully but finally, choosing Lye ahead of him. And she didn't have to strain to make the decision, he thought with a bitter humor. His proposition had struck her as foolish. He was a fat little peasant in her eyes, one of the anonymous people who tugged at their caps when she passed them by. When everything was quiet again, he thought, when the trouble with Retnick was over, then he'd think about fixing her and Lye. He said good-by without looking at her and left the room.

Sixteen

The ringing phone woke Retnick, and he sat up in the darkness and fumbled for his watch on the table beside the bed. The illuminated hands stood at six-thirty. He heard Mrs. Cara's door open, and then the cautious murmur of her voice. She knocked on his door a second or two later. Retnick crossed the floor and turned the knob., He had been dozing only a few minutes—except for a coat and tie he was fully dressed.

"It's a call for you," Mrs. Cara said.

Retnick nodded his thanks and went down the hall and picked up the receiver. "Hello?"

"Steve Retnick?" It was a girl's voice, low and intense.

"That's right."

"This is Dixie Davis." She laughed but the sound of it was all wrong. "I—I'm scared, I guess. That's why I called. You gave me your number, remember? A million years ago, I guess."

"Take it easy," he said.

"I got a call a few minutes ago. It was a man and he said he had dialed the wrong number. But it scared me. He hung up right away. It's so quiet here. The whole building is like a tomb. It's—nerves, I know. Isn't that right?"

"Did you call the police?"

"What for?" she said nervously. "I—I just wanted to talk to somebody, that's all. I know you think I'm no good, but a few minutes' talk won't corrupt you."

"I'll call the cops," Retnick said. "Now listen: lock your door and sit tight. Don't open up for anyone but a police officer. Watch the street from your windows and you'll see the squad car arrive. Understand?"

"You think I'm in trouble?"

"Why take chances? Keep that door locked, remember."

"All right, sure."

Retnick broke the connection and dialed the police board. He asked for the precinct which covered Dixie's neighborhood, and was put through to a Lieutenant Mynandahl. When he explained what the trouble was the lieutenant said, "All right," in an unexcited voice. "We'll send a car over to look into it. You say she heard a prowler?"

"That's right."

"We'll check it."

Retnick returned to his room, picked up his hat and coat, and left the house. It was black outside, and the streets were empty and cold. He headed for the avenue at a run, knowing that his chances for a cab were slim at this hour. He waited five minutes at the intersection, his collar turned up against the wind, until a cruiser turned off a cross-town street and pulled up for him. Retnick gave the driver Dixie's address and told him to hurry . . .

An empty, black-and-white squad car was pulled up before her building with the motor turning over smoothly. As Retnick paid off his driver he heard the metallic sound of the police radio, and the flat, businesslike voice of the announcer listing routine details and instructions. It was a comforting sound in the darkness and silence.

He went into the small foyer breathing more easily; the cops had got here ahead of him which meant there had been a very brief time-lag between her call and their arrival. Hardly time for anything to happen . . . Then he saw that the inner door stood slightly ajar and that the jamb had been worked on with a jimmy; splinters of torn wood gleamed whitely in the overhead light. Retnick hesitated, feeling the quickening beat of his heart. The cops might have forced their way in, which meant she hadn't answered their ring . . .

He took the steps two at a time and when he turned the

landing below her floor a hard young voice said, "Hold it right there. And get your hands up."

A uniformed patrolman stood at the top of the stairs and the gun in his hand was pointed at Retnick.

"I put the call in," Retnick said, standing perfectly still. "I talked to a Lieutenant Mynandahl and he said he'd send a car over here."

The cop said, "How'd you know there would be trouble?"

"She called me."

"All right, come on up," the cop said, after hesitating briefly.

Retnick knew then that he was too late. "She's dead, eh?"

"That's right. You go in and wait for the lieutenant. He'll want to talk to you."

Retnick walked down the short hallway to her apartment, noticing that here too the iron teeth of a jimmy had been at work on the wood above and below the door lock. Inside the neat living room a middle-aged cop was talking on the phone. He glanced at Retnick and a surprised little smile of recognition touched his round face. His name was Melburn, Retnick remembered; they had worked together in Harlem ten years ago.

Melburn waved to him and continued speaking into the phone. "We'll stick here until Homicide shows up," he said. "Right." Replacing the receiver he shook hands with Retnick and said, "Well, long time, eh? You know this girl?"

"Yes, I knew her," Retnick said slowly. And because of that she was dead, he thought. For the first time in five years he experienced something like guilt. "Where is she?"

"In the bathroom." Melburn shifted his weight awkwardly. "Steve, if she meant something to you, well I'm sorry."

Retnick shrugged wearily. "She didn't mean anything to me," he said. Turning he went to the bathroom and pushed open the door.

She looked even smaller in death, curled on the floor in a child's sleeping form, her knees drawn up almost to her chin. The bruises on her throat were partially concealed by the angle at which she lay, but he could see the mindless fear in her face, blurred and magnified by her swollen lips and widely staring eyes. One of her slippers had fallen off and her blue silk robe was twisted up around her thighs. The light above the medicine cabinet gleamed along her thin, chalk-white legs.

Retnick turned back to the living room and lit a cigarette. The smoke tasted hot and dry in his mouth. Melburn said, "We were cruising on Park when we got the call. We got here just a few minutes after it happened. Damn shame, eh?"

"It's a damn shame all right," Retnick said.

"You better stick around, I guess," Melburn said. "The detectives will want to talk to you."

Retnick pushed his hat back on his head and sat down on the edge of a chair with his big hands hanging limply between his knees. "I'll wait," he said. She had been sure that Evans would he get her, he was thinking. *Why did you put me on the spot?* That had been her question to him, and he hadn't bothered to answer it. He'd made a speech, he remembered. A pious angry speech. Well, why had he put her on the spot? Now it was an academic question. It was all I could do, he thought, drawing deeply on the cigarette. I had to make Evans think he was being framed. That someone was talking. Otherwise he'd never crack. It was Dixie's life against— He frowned, unable to complete the thought. Against what?

A Homicide detective named Caprizzio came in and Retnick stood and shook hands with him, relieved to get away from his pointless, guilty thoughts. He answered Caprizzio's questions, and Caprizzio nodded gloomily when he was through, and said, "These jobs that don't have a nickel's worth of planning in them are always the worst. The guy jimmies two doors, strangles her and walks out. That kind of murder is like a bolt of lightning, and just as hard to trace. Well, I'll see you around."

Retnick was ready to leave when the door opened and Lieutenant Neville came in, looking tired and worried. He frowned at Retnick and said, "Just a minute, I'll go with you," and then crossed the room and talked to Caprizzio for a few minutes.

Neville was very pale, Retnick noticed, and there was a hard look around his eyes. When he finished with Caprizzio he nodded to Retnick and said, "Let's go downstairs, Steve. I want to talk with you."

The darkness was lifting. A thin pearly light sparkled coldly on the frosted branches of the winter-black trees and shed a soft hazy glow along the well-kept little block. The wagon and three squads were double-parked along the curb, and a group of pedestrians, out early with their dogs, had bunched together across the street to watch the excitement. Two reporters and a photographer were waiting outside the foyer for Caprizzio's okay to go up; they all looked tired and irritable.

"What's going on?" one of them asked Neville. "Come on, don't be like Caprizzio the Cautious. Has she got any relatives in town? That's all the desk wants now. Pictures of her family, if any."

"It's not my case," Neville said. "Caprizzio will give you the works pretty soon, I imagine."

A uniformed patrolman put his head out the door. "Okay," he said to the reporters. "The lieutenant says you can come up."

Neville and Retnick walked down the sidewalk toward Park. The lieutenant took out his cigarettes, lit one and inhaled deeply. "I just left another dead one, Steve. Mario Amato. He blew his brains out an hour ago."

Retnick stared at him, and when he saw the expression on Neville's face the sense of guilt moved in him again, crowding insistently against the weight of his cold heavy anger. "When did this happen?" he asked.

They had stopped and were facing each other in the cold gray light of dawn. Neville said, "Anna Amato found him in bed when she got home from six o'clock Mass. She brought him a breakfast tray. Mario was in bed, a gun in his hand. Half his forehead was gone."

Retnick swallowed a dryness in his throat. "You're sure it's a suicide?"

"It's a suicide, all right."

I didn't kill him, Retnick thought. Mario had shot himself after being grilled by Neville. A soft, nervous kid, caught in a murder investigation, he'd taken the easy way out . . .

Neville stared at him with cold stern eyes. "I blame myself for this," he said. "Maybe you blame yourself, too. I don't know. We threw away the book and made a mess of things. It was your idea I carried out. I thought you deserved any break I could give you. But all we did was cause two deaths. The girl's murder, and Mario's suicide. My only consolation is that I didn't buy your insane notion to spread the word that Mario had squealed. If I had I might be responsible for another murder. But I didn't, and that's my one consolation. I wonder what yours is."

"You'll let Red Evans go now, I suppose?" Retnick said.

"We have nothing to hold him on. He's in the clear."

"You let him go," Retnick said slowly. "I'll be waiting for him."

"As a cop, I'm warning you," Neville said in a cold, official voice. "You get in trouble and I'll treat you like a lawbreaker."

"Thanks all to hell," Retnick said.

"Steve, I—" Neville paused, frowning into Retnick's hard face. "There's no way to get through to you," he said at last, and his voice was empty and tired. "But remember this: the price of vengeance can be too high for any man to pay. You'll know that someday."

"I'll pay it, don't worry," Retnick said.

Neville shrugged. The instant of compassion was gone and his face was once again closed and grim. "Good night, Steve," he said shortly, and walked down the quiet street to the police cars.

Seventeen

By noon Nick Amato's home had become a place of well-organized grief and mourning. His wife's friends filled the house, moving solemnly about their duties with funeral expressions on their work-worn faces. There was little they could do to comfort Anna; she lay in bed, turning her head slowly from side to side, pressing Mario's first communion picture tightly to her breasts. She had passed from hysteria to shock; her expression was dazed and incredulous and only at infrequent intervals did tears start in her dull brown eyes. Her friends murmured their sympathies to her and left her room with handkerchiefs pressed to their eyes. Time would help her, they knew. Nothing else. Meanwhile there was work to be done; the house to be cleaned from top to bottom, the plans made for marketing and cooking. The men who came to the wake would need to eat and drink. Nothing ever changed that.

Nick Amato sat in the kitchen, a dead cigar in his hand and a cup of hot coffee before him on the table. He was tired and nervous; his face was gray with fatigue and there was a tiny but annoying tremor in his left eyelid. The knowledge that he was safe hadn't put him at ease, for some reason. With Mario and the girl dead he was safe, but he couldn't relax; every sound in the house grated on his quivering nerves, and there was a cold, painful ache in the pit of his stomach.

Joe Lye stood with his back to the window, smoking a cigarette with quick, hungry drags. Occasionally he glanced at the ceiling, in the direction of Anna's room. "She's calmed down," he said, drawing a deep breath.

"Don't talk about it," Amato said.

A stout gray-haired woman opened the door without knocking. "Father Bristow is here," she said to Amato. "He's gone up to see Anna."

"That's good," Amato said, and stared at her until she smiled nervously and closed the door.

Lye rubbed both hands over his face. "You think he can help her?" he said.

"Anna will listen to him," Amato said. "He'll tell her it was God's will. He'll tell her to be brave."

"What would he tell her if he knew the truth?"

"Don't talk about it, I said."

"That's easy for you."

"Shut up!" Amato said, glaring at him. "It had to be done. Connors told me he'd spilled something to the cops. Supposing he squealed that I told him to hire Evans? It had to be this way, Joe. He could hurt me. Like I can hurt you."

Lye rubbed a fist over his tight mouth. He stood indecisively for a moment, and then pulled out a chair and sat down at the table facing Amato. "We're going to talk," he said. "I got something to say to you."

Amato shrugged. "Go ahead."

"Kay told me about the deal you offered her."

"Women are funny, Joe. You pay 'em a compliment that don't mean anything and they think you're serious." There was a purpose in Lye that Amato didn't understand; but his intuition told him it was dangerous. "So why worry about the funny ideas a woman gets, Joe?" He smiled slowly but his eyes were wary and alert.

"That's not the important thing," Lye said. "So she misunderstood you. Okay. What I'm talking about is you and me, Nick. I'm going to work *with* you from now on, not for you. You understand?"

"You got a gripe, I guess. Keep talking, Joe."

"When we take over Glencannon's local, I'm going to run it," Lye said. "You and I will split up this stretch of the docks. We'll be partners."

Amato dropped his cigar into his coffee and it went out with an angry little hiss. "Joe, I don't like partners," he said gently. "You know that by now. Joe Ventra wanted to be a partner, remember?"

"You remember something now," Lye said, in a tight, straining voice. "Kay is ready to swear she heard you tell me to kill your nephew. You better remember that good. We'll go to the cops—Kay and me—and that will put you right in the chair."

Amato smiled faintly. "That would put you in the chair too, Joe."

"It's a standoff," Lye said. "You got the Donaldson rap hanging over me, I got the kid's murder on you. So we're partners, Nick. You ain't going to needle and hound me about going back to jail. If you do you'll pay a high price for your fun."

Amato kept his anger in check. He raised his eyebrows in a little gesture of good-humored resignation. "I'm a sensible fellow," he said. "You can hurt me, I can hurt you. So it figures we should be friends."

"Partners," Lye said.

Amato shrugged and smiled. "Partners."

Lye rubbed a hand over his damp forehead. He could hardly believe that he'd won; it had taken all his courage to do this, and now he was so spent and drained that his hands were shaking. But he had never known such relief. Already the tense and clotted fear of Amato was easing out of him, and he was suddenly sure that the violent crimson nightmares would never haunt his sleep again. There would be an end to the smothering horror, to the taste of shame in his mouth, as he climbed with agonizing slowness to sanity and consciousness. And the tic that afflicted his face, that sinister barometer of his passions, even that might disappear. Without fear, anything was possible. He was almost grateful to Amato now. "I swear, Nick, we'll get along fine," he said. "You're still the boss. But I had to get out from under you. Kay and I want some kind of life together. We want to live like normal people."

"That's what you want, eh?"

"Everybody does, I guess."

"Maybe you're right." Amato looked at the dead stump of his cigar floating in the coffee. "You know, Joe, she was out of the room when I told you to take care of Mario. She didn't hear nothing."

Lye felt his lips tightening. "She'll swear she heard it all," he said.

"Oh sure. I was just thinking. You can't be normal people." He looked at Lye and smiled. "You're too smart."

"That's a good thing to remember, Nick."

"Don't worry. I'll remember it," Amato said. He stood up then and rubbed his stomach. "I better go up with Anna."

"Okay, Nick. I'll be at the local if you need me."

When he had gone Amato stood for a minute or so staring at the door. He heard Anna's friends moving about above him on the second floor, and from the street the faint noise of children playing. At last he sat down and rubbed both hands over his face, drawing a black curtain over reality for a brief welcome moment. His body felt slack and hot and his left eye was quivering with fatigue. He knew he was in trouble; the knowledge was intuitive but certain. There was Retnick and Neville, and now Joe Lye. They were forcing him to move, prodding him into action, not giving him time to think. That was how they got you; by making you jump. Finally you jumped one time too many . . .

Amato went down the hallway and got into his heavy overcoat. He heard Father Bristow's voice at the top of the stairs, and he let himself out quickly; he didn't want to talk to the priest now. It was one thing with the old woman, listening to them say how terrible it was that the boy was dead, but the priest was different. He looked right through you; Amato knew he had never fooled him for a minute.

The day was cold and overcast with heavy dark clouds. In the steel-gray light the bitter colors of the street were more

dismal than usual. The street was dirty, and the black iron
fire escapes crawled like a rusty growth up the faces of the
mud-colored brownstones. Amato walked slowly to the
waterfront, not quite sure why he had left the house. He
looked through the fog and saw the terminal his local controlled, a long square finger poking into the gray river. Five
hundred men, coopers, checkers, truckers, winch operators,
laborers—they paid him to work there. The jobs were safe
as long as they stayed in line. That used to mean something
to him, but today it seemed flat and pointless.

After a few minutes he turned and started slowly back to
his house, to the black-shawled old women and the gloom
that permeated every room. But it had to be faced.

The priest had gone, one of the women told him as he
hung up his overcoat. He would be back tonight.

"That's good," Amato said. He looked at the woman until
she bobbed her head at him and retreated toward the kitchen.
Then, sighing heavily, he picked up the phone and gave the
operator a number.

Connors sounded sleepy and irritable, but his manner
changed instantly when he recognized Amato's voice.

"I just turned in," he said. "It was quite a long night."

"I'm going to make a hero out of you," Amato said,
staring down the dark hallway to the kitchen. "You're going
to solve that old Donaldson killing all by yourself. You'll
have the evidence and you'll make the pinch tonight. You'll
like being a hero, won't you?"

Connors' laugh was strained. "It's a role I play pretty
well. What's the rest of it, Nick?"

"They guy you arrest don't like it," Amato said quietly.
"He puts up a fight, breaks for it maybe. And you got to
shoot him."

"Nick, there's been too much of it lately," Connors said,
his voice rising nervously. "A month from now would be—"

"Shut up! You're going to be a hero or you're going to
be in jail." Amato rubbed his forehead. He was jumping
now, without time to think. It happened to the smartest

guys. They jumped for safety and landed in trouble. But there wasn't time to think.

"Sure, Nick," Connors said hastily. "I'll handle it, you know that. I only thought the timing was awkward."

"The timing is right," Amato said.

"Okay. Who is it?"

"Joe Lye," Amato said, and put the receiver carefully back in place.

Eighteen

It was eight o'clock that night when Retnick rang the bell of his wife's apartment. He had spent the day in his room trying fruitlessly to find a solution to his problem. It was a moral problem, he had decided irritably, one his Jesuit teachers would have had a field day examining. Take what you want and pay the price! That had made sense to him. But he was beginning to realize that it wasn't as simple as that. If you couldn't pay the price, then what? It wasn't a clean exchange; you didn't make the payment and put an end to it . . .

He heard her light footsteps. Then she opened the door and looked up at him uncertainly. She wore a white silk blouse with black slacks, and her hair was tied up behind her head in a pony-tail. He noticed that she carried two freshly ironed blouses over her arm.

"You didn't say when you were leaving," he said. "I—I wanted to say good-bye."

"I'm taking a flight at ten," she said. "I was just packing. I'm glad you could stop by."

"You're busy, I guess."

"No, I'm practically through."

Retnick entered the room and turned his hat around awkwardly in his hands. There were no easy words. Everything seemed to come out with an effort. "You go ahead and finish packing," he said. "Take your time."

"All right, I won't be long."

When the door closed behind her Retnick looked around at the familiar furniture and pictures. She hadn't changed things. His big chair was in the same place, and his pipe rack was still on the table. She'd added a new picture or two, and a bookcase had been built in beside the fireplace. That was about all.

He sat down on a large ottoman without removing his overcoat and rubbed a hand across his forehead. Something was wrong with him, he knew.

When she opened the door he stood quickly.

"Please sit down," she said. "Would you like a cup of coffee?"

"No, I'm fine."

"How about a drink?"

"Never mind."

She sat down on the sofa, tucking her feet beneath her, and lit a cigarette. For a moment or two they were silent, and then Retnick said heavily, "Do you have to go tonight? I mean is there any need to rush?"

"No, not particularly. But I'd like to get settled down a bit before I start work."

"Sure," he said pointlessly. She was a million miles from him, he realized, cool and distant, unmoved by his presence. There was no fear or anxiety in her eyes, no tentative appeal in her manner. She wasn't unhappy in a positive way, she was simply impassive; he knew he didn't touch her any more.

"I want to talk to you," he said, turning and looking into the fireplace. "Will you listen a minute?"

"Of course, Steve."

"Put off your trip," he said. "Stay here until I finish the job I've got to do."

"What would be the point of that?"

"I don't know," he said wearily. "Maybe there's no point to it. But it might make things different. With me anyway. Maybe I could see things in a different light. That's all I'm asking you to take a chance on."

"It's a pretty slim chance, I'm afraid."

"Maybe it is. But it's the only one I can offer you."

"I'm sorry, Steve," she said.

He looked at her then, jarred by the almost casual tone of her voice. "You won't do it?" he said.

"There wouldn't be any point to it," she said, glancing up at him. "I might as well be honest, Steve. You—you've turned into something—well, it doesn't matter. Maybe you were that kind of a man all the time. I don't know.'' She shurgged lightly. ''You think I had a fine roistering time of it while you were away. But for the record they were five miserable years. I was scared most of the time. Scared because I couldn't understand the cruel and stupid pride that made you refuse to let me help you. Did you stop to wonder what that did to me?'' She shook her head as he started to speak. ''It's not worth arguing about. But I'd like to finish this, please. You told me to get a divorce, you refused to see me, and then you behaved like a madman because there was someone else while you were gone.'' She smiled sadly. ''And my big affair, my great sin! He sang at the club for a while. He was a gentle young man who drank too much and could have written a big book about loneliness. It lasted a month. And that was enough to convince me you were worth waiting for, even if it took fifty years instead of five. I regretted it, I made what amends I could, and I settled down to wait. That's how I put in my five-year stretch, with an occasional dinner with the Ragonis, or a drink with Lieutenant Neville. I might as well have been in jail, too.''

If she was angry or bitter, Retnick thought, it would be different. But she seemed disinterested and slightly weary.

"You didn't care about my pride or peace of mind," she went on, studying him thoughtfully with her wide gray eyes. "That's what I couldn't understand. But now I believe you don't care about anybody. You want to kill the men who framed you. And some day you will. You'll be the final judge on that score. Just as you're the final judge on my morals. You're the final arbiter on all behavior, all questions of right and wrong. What you say goes! Well, it doesn't go with me, Steve. I can think of nothing less pleasing than

living with you and wondering what suspicions were crop-
ping up in your mind and what action you were planning
to take. You—"

"All right," he said, rubbing a hand over his forehead.
"I get the general idea."

The phone in the bedroom began to ring and she turned
away from him quickly.

"Just a minute," he said. "This man, the singer." He
hesitated, frowning. "Did he love you?"

"Why do you ask that?"

"I don't know. Never mind."

She looked at him and he saw that her lips were trembling;
his question had pierced her cool indifference. The phone
rang again and she said, "Excuse me," in a small, unsteady
voice.

When she returned to the room he was staring into the
fireplace, a dark frown on his face. "It's for you," she said.

He turned to her, still frowning. "Are you sure?"

"Yes. She asked for you."

He shrugged and walked into the cool, softly lighted bedroom. A gray tweed suit and a lace-edged slip were laid
out on the bed, and a pair of brown leather pumps were on
the floor beside two pieces of luggage. The room smelled
faintly of the lavender sachets she kept with her gloves and
lingerie. Retnick sighed and picked up the phone. "This is
Steve Retnick."

"My name is Kay Johnson. You don't know me, but I'm
Joe—I'm a friend of Joe Lye's." The woman's voice was
low and controlled, but he could hear a tremor of fear running
under it.

"I'm not very much interested in Joe Lye's friends," he
said.

"Please listen to me. Please! I know you don't care anything about him—" She stopped and drew a deep, quivering
breath. "No one cares about him! He's just a cheap little
hoodlum with a twisted face. I know that!"

"What did you want?" Retnick said. She was almost hysterical, he knew; the tight control of her voice was slipping.

"He's going to be killed," she said. "Nick Amato is going to kill him!"

"You'd better call the police if you're worried about him," Retnick said.

"I can't! The police are going to kill him. Don't you understand?"

"Calm down a bit. You said it was Amato."

"Amato sent a police officer to do it. That's how he works."

"Was it a man named Connors?" Retnick asked her sharply.

"Yes, that's his name. He's going to kill Joe."

"Why did you call me?"

"I don't know. Joe told me you hated Amato. So I looked you up in the book. They're afraid of you."

"And you want me to save your boy friend?"

"No, it wasn't that," she said, laughing softly. "No one can save Joe. The poor guy is all through. But nothing can save Amato."

Retnick's hand tightened on the receiver. "What's that?"

"I can hang him," she said. "I can give you his head on a platter. Are you interested?"

"Where are you now?"

She gave him the address of her apartment, still laughing softly, and Retnick said, "You sit tight. I'll be along in ten or fifteen minutes."

Then he broke the connection and dialed the Thirty-First. Waiting for Neville he turned her story around in his mind. If she were telling the truth there must have been a major row between Amato and Lye. But over what?

When Neville answered, Retnick said, "Lieutenant, this is Retnick. Wait until I finish before you tell me to go to hell. I just had a call from a woman named Kay Johnson, Joe Lye's girl friend. She tells me Amato has put the finger on Lye, and she says she can hang Amato. Whether she's got anything on him or not, I don't know. But I thought I'd let you know. I'm going to her apartment now."

Neville took a deep breath and swore irritably. "Where

does she live?" he said at last.

Retnick told him and Neville said, "All right. Meet me in front of her place. I'll leave here now."

Retnick put the phone down and walked slowly into the living room. Marcia looked at him and said, "You sounded excited. I hope it's good news."

"Yes, it's good news," Retnick said. He picked up his hat and she came with him to the door. With his hand on the knob he looked down at her and said, "This could be the end of it. Tonight could end it."

"I hope you'll have what you want then."

He stared into her small familiar face, silently turning the painful thoughts in his mind. Then he said awkwardly, "I thought you'd be better off with a divorce. I thought you would get started over without me. I couldn't let you visit me in jail." He shrugged his big shoulders. "I wasn't built to be a monkey in a cage. And I couldn't come back to you as a jailbird. It was the way I felt about you. You were like some prize I'd won by a fluke, and I couldn't crawl back to you—" He gestured helplessly. "I had to prove I was framed."

"You never had to prove anything to me, Steve," she said. "You still don't." She touched his arm gently. "Stay here and talk to me until I have to go. Let Lieutenant Neville finish this job tonight. You've done enough."

"But it's not over yet," he said. "I've got to finish it."

"You want to finish it," she said, sighing and taking her hand from his arm. "It isn't clearing your name, coming back to me like a white and shining knight. Be honest, Steve. You want to be in at the kill."

"Maybe that's it," he said. Nothing made sense any more, he thought, watching her with a faint and bitter smile. "You're still planning to leave, of course?"

"There's nothing here for me," she said. "I'll be on the ten o'clock flight."

"Well, good luck," he said.

"Thanks. And take care of yourself, Steve."

"Sure," he said heavily, and opened the door.

She watched him from the doorway as he walked down the hall. He rang for the elevator and stood with his back to her looking down at the floor. The building was still and silent. When the elevator arrived he stepped into it without looking back. She waved tentatively but he was already out of sight. The doors closed on him with a dry and final ring.

Nineteen

Lieutenant Neville was waiting for Retnick in front of Kay Johnson's apartment building. There was an obvious constraint in his manner as he greeted him and said, "What do you think this woman has on Amato?"

"I told you she wasn't specific."

"It's probably dynamite," Neville said, throwing his cigarette aside. "She probably knows he played hooky in third grade."

"Then why did you bother coming over?"

Neville glanced up and down the dark street, a humorless grin touching his hard lips. "I'll be damned if I know," he said. "Let's go up."

Kay Johnson opened the door and smiled nervously from Neville to Retnick. She wore a simple black dress with pearls, and she had obviously prepared herself carefully for this role; her make-up was fresh, and her shining blonde hair was meticulously in place. But all the careful grooming wasn't enough to conceal the fear in her eyes and the lines of tension about her mouth.

Neville sensed her anxiety and said quietly, "Miss Johnson, I'm a police officer. My name is Lieutenant Neville. This is Steve Retnick whom you talked with on the phone a short while ago. May we come in?"

"Yes, yes of course," she said quickly. She was looking at Retnick. "I—I didn't know you'd call the police."

"It's better this way, believe me," he said.

Neville glanced around the gracefully furnished room with professional interest. Then he looked at Kay Johnson and said, "What have you got to tell us?"

She sat down on the sofa, so slowly that it seemed the strength was draining from her legs. "Nick Amato is going to kill Joe Lye," she said.

"How do you know that?" Neville said casually.

"Amato sent a detective here, a man named Connors. He rang the bell, I don't know, around eight, I think. Joe was in the kitchen then, but Connors didn't ask to see him. He told me to stay in the living room and he went through the apartment with his gun out. He opened the closet here in the foyer and then started for the bedroom. Maybe Joe saw him coming—I don't know. Maybe he heard him talking to me. Anyway, when this man, Connors, reached the kitchen the back door was open and Joe was gone. I—knew from the way Connors looked and acted that he was going to kill Joe the minute he saw him."

"What did Connors do then?" Neville said.

"He swore at me, he seemed very nervous. Then he went down the back stairs after Joe."

"Did he say he was going to kill Lye?"

She shook her head slowly. "I could tell from the way he acted."

Neville glanced at Retnick and the lack of expression on his face was eloquent. "From the way he acted, eh? Well, do you know *why* Amato wants Lye murdered?"

She seemed puzzled by the question. "Of course," she said. "I—I thought you'd know that, too."

Neville sighed. "We know very little, Miss Johnson."

"Why is Amato going to have Lye killed?" Retnick said, wetting his lips. He could guess the answer, and the knowledge was a guilty terrible weight in his breast.

"Mario Amato didn't commit suicide," she said, taking a deep unsteady breath. "He was killed. Joe killed him." Turning away from them she put a hand to her forehead and began to weep silently. "Amato made Joe kill him.

Because Mario talked to the police."

Neville looked sharply at Retnick. Then he sat down beside her and took her shoulders in his hands. "Did you hear Amato tell Joe Lye to kill Mario?"

She hesitated a second or two, and in the silence Retnick could hear the labored, despairing beat of his heart. She was going to lie, he knew, but that didn't matter; she knew the truth. "Yes, I heard him tell Joe," she said, raising her eyes and staring into Neville's eyes. "It was right in this room."

"Will you put that in a statement?" Neville said. "Will you repeat it in court?"

"I'll shout it at the top of my lungs," she said, leaning against him and shaking her head as if she were in pain. "He made Joe do it. And now he's going to kill Joe. He's got to pay for that."

"He'll pay," Neville said. He looked up at Retnick. "Get her coat," he said quietly. "We can hang Amato for murder with a little luck."

"Sure," Retnick said, rubbing his forehead. Turning quickly he went to the closet near the front door. A half-a-dozen coats hung there and he pulled one down without even looking at it. We'll hang Amato, he thought, as the cruel guilty pressure grew within him. But who'll hang me?

They drove in silence across town to the Thirty-First. Neville took Kay Johnson inside to give a preliminary statement, and Retnick waited alone in the car, trying fruitlessly to evade his dark, accusing thoughts. But there was no escape; no matter how he twisted and dodged they clung to him.

He didn't hear the doors of the precinct open and he started when Kleyburg cried, "Steve! You said it wouldn't happen."

Retnick turned and saw the old detective standing on the sidewalk beside the car, staring down at him with wide, frightened eyes. He had come out without a coat and the cold wind had blown his thin gray hair into a tangle over his forehead. "You said it wouldn't happen," he cried again.

Retnick got out of the car quickly and took Kleyburg's shoulders in his hands. "Go back inside," he said. "You'll catch pneumonia out here."

"I heard Neville talking to that woman," Kleyburg said, pulling free from Retnick's hands. "Mario was murdered. We killed him, Steve."

A patrolman coming on duty looked at them curiously, then shrugged and went into the station.

"Not so loud," Retnick said, wetting his lips. He couldn't meet the pain and confusion in the old man's eyes. "Mario was in on it. He deserved killing."

"There was no evidence. Just your say-so. And we killed him on the strength of that."

"Miles, you're wrong. Tomorrow it will look different to you."

Kleyburg shook his head slowly. The confusion and anxiety seemed to fall away from him; he looked at Retnick as if he could suddenly see him very, very clearly. "It won't be different in the morning," he said. "I told you I never had any trouble looking at myself in a mirror. Well, that's over. After forty-two years as a cop I wind up a murderer. That won't change in the morning. For you or for me, Steve."

"Miles—"

Another voice cut coldly and sharply through the silence. "So you used Kleyburg, eh, Steve?"

Retnick looked up quickly and saw Lieutenant Neville standing on the steps of the precinct, his pale face an angry vivid slash against the darkness. "I wouldn't help, so you made an old man do it," he said, walking slowly down to the sidewalk.

"It paid off," Retnick said, in a tight, unnatural voice. "We've got Amato."

"And that's all that matters, eh? Pay off your scores! To hell with everything else." Neville stared at Kleyburg and a touch of compassion gradually softened the lines of his face. "I heard it all, Miles," he said. "You'd better leave your gun and badge on my desk and go on home. We'll talk this over in the morning. If it turns out the kid was guilty we can square it."

"You can't square it," Kleyburg said, looking into the darkness and shaking his head wearily. "It's not a thing you can fix by juggling a report or two around." Then he turned to the lieutenant, and his eyes were helpless and pleading. "I didn't want to pull this deal."

"I understand," Neville said, staring at Retnick. He drew a deep breath. "Okay, Steve. We can pick up Amato now. You got what you wanted."

"That's right," Retnick said, not feeling much of anything at all. "I got what I wanted. . . ."

It was nine-fifteen when they arrived at Nick Amato's home. A line of cars were double-parked before the house, and a group of men stood on the sidewalk smoking cigars and talking in low voices. A crepe hung on the door, gleaming dully in the light that streamed from the inner hallway through the transom window. Neville nodded to the men and went up the stairs. They murmured indistinct greetings and watched him cautiously as he entered the house with Retnick. Then they came together and talked softly among themselves.

Retnick removed his hat and followed Neville into the softly lighted parlor. Floral pieces were banked on three sides of the room; a space along the windows had been left clear for the casket, which hadn't as yet arrived from the funeral home. A half-dozen men and women were present, their faces grave and sad, and Father Bristow was standing in the archway that led to the dining room. Anna Amato sat in a straight chair facing the space the casket would occupy. She wore a heavy black silk dress and her hands lay limply in her lap, palms turned upward in an unconscious gesture of entreaty. There was no expression on her dark, tear-swollen face, but her head was turned slightly to one side, defensively and helplessly, as if she were expecting a blow.

"Excuse me, Mrs. Amato," Neville said.

Father Bristow came forward casually, but his eyes were sharp and interested. Standing behind Anna, he put his hands on her soft round shoulders and watched the lieutenant.

"It was good of you to come," Anna said, without looking up.

"I'm Lieutenant Neville. I'm sorry your son is dead. But I came to see your husband on an important matter. Is he here?"

Anna made a weary little gesture with one hand. "He has gone out."

"Do you know where he went?"

"No."

"Or when he'll be back?"

"I know nothing," Anna said, shaking her head slowly. She seemed hardly conscious of Neville's questions. Two of the men present came and stood beside the priest and looked at the lieutenant with unfriendly eyes. "My son is dead," Anna said, rising to her feet wearily and awkwardly. Tears started in her eyes as she stared hopelessly at Neville. "They bring his body home soon. Can't you let me wait for him in peace?"

"I'm sorry to disturb you, Mrs. Amato," Neville said.

Father Bristow said, "Couldn't this wait, lieutenant?"

"I think so," Neville said.

Anna Amato suddenly shook her fists in the air, sensing that in some way the sanctity of her grief had been violated. "This is a house of death," she cried, staring at Neville and Retnick with burning eyes. "I wait for my son. I know nothing of my husband. I know nothing except that my son is dead."

"I'm sorry," Neville said gently. "Let's go, Steve."

"Wait a minute," Retnick said, staring at Amato's wife with bitter eyes. "You don't know anything, eh? Nobody knows anything about Nick Amato. They don't see anything, hear anything, or say anything."

"Steve!" Father Bristow said sharply.

"It's time you learned something then," Retnick said, still staring at Amato's wife. "Your son didn't commit suicide.

Joe Lye killed him. And Nick Amato gave the orders. That's why the cops are here now."

A stocky man in a black suit swore softly and surged against Retnick, but he might as well have tried to knock down a brick wall with his fists. Retnick shoved him halfway across the room with a blow of his arm. He was breathing slowly and heavily; a bursting pain filled his breast as he stared into the horror in Anna Amato's eyes. "Now you know something," he said thickly.

The room was still as death as Anna turned slowly and awkwardly to Neville. She strained for breath as her eyes searched his face. "Is that true?" she said in a dry whisper. "You say this, too?"

Neville looked away from her and wet his lips. Anna wheeled with a cry of pain and caught Father Bristow's arm in her hands. "They lie, they lie," she said in a sharp loud voice. "Tell me they lie."

"Sit down, Anna," Father Bristow said. "There will be time for this later." He stared coldly at Retnick. "This isn't the time for it. Not now. Not in this house."

Anna turned slowly from him, her lips trembling with silent words. Then she sat down heavily and began to shake her head from side to side. "No one says he lies," she muttered. "No one says he lies."

"I'm not lying," Retnick said, forcing the words out with an effort.

"I said I know nothing," Anna said, smiling softly and emptily. "But it isn't true. For thirty years I watch and see, I listen and hear. I know everything."

Retnick turned sharply and walked to the front door. Outside, in the cold darkness, he lit a cigarette with trembling fingers and then ran the back of his hand over his forehead. The men who had been standing in front of the house were gone; the street was empty and silent. Retnick breathed deeply but he couldn't seem to get enough air. His anger was gone, everything seemed to be gone, and he felt nothing but a cold, draining impotence . . .

It was a few minutes later when Father Bristow came out

of the house and walked slowly down the stairs. He looked at Retnick and said, "Did you have to do it that way, Steve?"

"It had to be done," Retnick said. "So I did it."

"She'll never get over it," Father Bristow said.

Retnick glanced at him and it was then the priest saw the change in his eyes. "Neither will I," Retnick said. "Doesn't that make us even?"

Father Bristow sighed and said quietly, "I just don't know, Steve."

Neville came out a little later. He said, "She wasn't kidding when she said she knew something. Amato's on the run. He left here half an hour ago. And she knows where he's running to. I'll call the district from the car and get some help. Good night, Father."

As Neville stepped on the starter of his car a police squad turned into the block and roared toward them under full power.

"I'll see what's up," Neville said. He stepped from the car and walked toward the young patrolman who had climbed from the squad. Retnick watched as the two men talked for perhaps half a minute, and then the partolman saluted and Neville walked quickly back to the car. His face was pale and drawn in the yellow glare of the headlights. Climbing in beside Retnick, he turned the ignition key and stepped on the starter. Then he let out his breath slowly and settled back in the seat. He looked at Retnick with an odd expression on his face; there was anger in the set of his mouth, but his eyes were sad and bewildered. "I warned you, Steve," he said heavily. "I warned you the best way I knew. I told you sometimes there's a price to vengeance that no man can pay. Now you've run up a big bill."

"What's the matter?" Retnick said sharply, as a strange chill went through his body.

"After we left the Thirty-First Kleyburg went down in the basement and tried to kill himself," Neville said. "He's still alive but it doesn't look good."

Retnick rubbed the back of his fist cruelly over his mouth. "Where did they take him?" he muttered. "I want to see him. I've got to seem him before he dies."

"You wanted to get Amato," Neville said. "Let's finish that job." He looked at Retnick and sighed. Then he said gently, "You can't help Miles now, Steve."

"Sure," Retnick said heavily. "I can't help him, I can't help anybody."

Twenty

Amato sat stiffly beside the driver and watched the heavy concrete support of the elevated highway flash past them into the darkness. Twelfth Avenue stretched ahead of him, a black, wind-swept tunnel into which the car's headlights bored like thick yellow lances. A small leather suitcase rested on his lap, and his arms were wrapped around it, hugging it tightly against his body. Under the black brim of his hat his cold brown eyes were tense and worried. This was the last big jump. If he slipped now it was all over.

"Everything is set, eh?" he said to the driver for pehaps the fifth time.

"Sure, there's nothing to worry about," the driver said casually. He was a short, slender man with graying hair and features that were pinched together into an expression of foxy good humor.

"I better not have to worry," Amato said. "I don't pay money to have things go wrong."

"It was short notice, Mr. Amato," the driver said. "We done our best. The launch is waiting at Pier 17. The guard there left a door open and took a walk for himself. You'll go down the Hudson, through the Narrows and over to Sheepshead Bay. I didn't get a final check yet, but the fishing boat is supposed to be there with two men to run it. The trip to Cuba takes a week. After that we're out of it."

"I got things set in Cuba," Amato said. "I had that set a long time."

"Well, we done our best on this end," the driver said philosophically. "You got to be lucky, though."

"You better hope I'm lucky," Amato said, glancing at him with his awkward little smile.

"We done our best," the driver said. Some of the good humor left his face as he felt Amato's eyes on him. Most men on the run were at the mercy of those who helped them; they could only pay and pray. But Nick Amato wasn't like most men. If this thing went wrong the driver knew that the waterfront would be a very unhealthy place for him.

Amato stared straight ahead again and hugged the grip to his chest. Instinct had made him run. There were men who would have stood fast and fought, betting on themselves, betting on money, influence, lawyers. But Amato had a peasant's instinct for survival. He fled without regret, as he would have fled from a volcano that threatened his village. Maybe he would come back some day. But he didn't think about this. Now it was important to get to Cuba and from there to Naples. He carried the harvest of thirty violent but profitable years in his suitcase, and in Naples he could live comfortably, and perhaps think about coming back. Amato needed time to think, and he was buying that as much as safety.

The car slowed to a stop in the darkness before Pier 17's vast silent warehouse. "Well, here you are," the driver said, letting the motor idle. "The door is unlocked, the guard is a couple of blocks away having a cup of coffee. The motor launch is tied up at the end of the terminal waiting for you. Okay?"

"It better be okay," Amato said. "If nothing goes wrong I'll send you a bottle of *Lacryma Christi* from Naples."

"We'll appreciate that, Mr. Amato."

Amato grunted and got out of the car. The driver nodded at him, his face a thin pale blur in the darkness, and then started up toward Ninth Street. Amato stood in the darkness

watching the red tail-light until it disappeared at the intersection. He was suddenly aware of the silence; it stretched
out on all sides of him, spreading hungrily to those distant
places where there was noise and laughter and life. He was
alone on the little island of sound that was bounded by the
rapid beat of his heart. Turning abruptly he walked to the
warehouse. The small door used by the guard was open; a
light from inside drew a thin bright line along the edge of
the jamb. Amato pushed the door in cautiously. A single
bulb gleamed in the checker's office, spreading a circle of
brightness around the entrance to the warehouse.

But beyond this small yellow pool the terminal was lost
in a vast echoing darkness. The launch waited for him at
the end of this black cavern, the first link in the chain that
would pull him to safety.

Amato closed the little door behind him, breathing more
easily. A hundred-yard walk and he was on his way. He
shifted the heavy suitcase to his right hand, tugged unneces-
sarily at his hat brim and started into the shadows.

And one of them began to move.

A little cry of terror broke through Amato's lips. He
backed toward the door, feeling the sickening speed of his
heartbeat, and tasting the strong bitter fear in his mouth.
Something darker than the shadows was coming toward him
silently.

He saw the gleam of black shoes and they stepped into
the yellow light, and then a voice he knew said, "The trip
is off, Nick. It ends here." Joe Lye came out of the darkness,
his face pale and tense above the narrow black cylinder of
his body. One side of his mouth was pulled up in an unnatural, ghastly smile, and a gun glinted in his hand. "You
should have taken me for a partner," he said. "That way
you wouldn't have to die."

"Joe, you gave me a scare," Amato said, trying desperately to smile. "I—I been looking for you. We got to clear
out, you and me. I waited as long as I could—but it's all
right now." He heard the hysterical note in his voice, but
he couldn't help himself. "I got plenty of dough here. And

the boat's waiting. For you and me. We got to go, Joe."

"You weren't looking for me," Lye said. "Connors was looking for me. You shouldn't have used a punk like him on a tough job, Nick. That's the biggest mistake you made."

"Joe, we got no time for talking," Amato said, trying to swallow the dry constriction in his throat. He dropped the grip and locked his hands together in a desperate appeal. "We're making Cuba the first stop, Joe. I got everything set. Passports, dough, berths on a freighter. It's all set for you and me. You'll like it there. It's hot but the breezes are cool. And they make drinks with rum and lots of lime. It's great, Joe." There was a high giddy tremble in Amato's voice now, and his smile stretched the skin whitely across his cheek bones. "What d'ye say, Joe? I look after things good, eh? And when we get to Italy I show you a fine time. Up in Milan they got night clubs and restaurants just like here. But we got to get moving. You carry the dough." He laughed shrilly. "That's right, you carry the dough. Nick trusts you."

"You're not going to Cuba," Lye said in a cold, empty voice. "You gave Connors that Donaldson rap. That finished me. Now I'm going to finish you. You forgot I knew about this pier, eh?"

"Joe, you're crazy," Amato shouted. "I always did the thinking, didn't I? You do what I say and we'll make it to Naples."

"Just a few seconds, that's all you got," Lye said in the same empty voice. "You used to wonder why I prayed in the death cell. Now you can find out."

"Joe, be smart! We got a whole life ahead of us. With dough and—"

A dry metallic click sounded as Lye cocked the gun. "You're wasting time," he said. "Here you go, Nick."

"Joe!" Amato screamed. He fell on his knees and clasped his hands over his breast. "Don't shoot me. Give me a break."

"So long, Nick."

"God—" Amato's voice was an incredulous whisper. He

knew then that he was going to die—here in this cold
warehouse, with a satchel of money at his feet and the
launch that could take him to safety moored only a hundred
yards away. He stared at Lye, while a desolate, hopeless
fear spread sluggishly through his body. "God I'm sorry—"
His voice broke there; the words of the Act of Contrition
spun in his head, eluding his desperate search. "I'm sorry,"
he said, beginning to weep. "I didn't do wrong. There was
no other way—because I dread the loss of Heaven." He
groped frantically for the familiar words. "And the pain of
Hell. With your help, I amend my life." That was all. He
stared through his tears at Lye and shook his head slowly.

"Who were you praying to?" Lye said bitterly, and shot
him twice just below the heart.

The echoes of the report rang through the immense warehouse, racing each other in noisy confusion toward the river.
And above this clamoring racket Lye heard the keening wail
of police sirens.

For an instant he stood perfectly still, the gun hanging
limply at his side. A small, perplexed frown touched his
forehead as he looked down at Amato. "Nick," he whispered, "can you hear it? It's cops."

But Amato didn't answer him; he lay on his back staring
in fear and wonder at the shadows closing slowly over his
eyes. His breathing was shallow and rapid, a laboring painful
sound in the silence.

Lye looked around uncertainly. Then, moving with jerky
strides, he picked up the grip that lay beside Amato, and
ran into the darkness of the terminal. Ahead of him was the
river and the launch. This wasn't part of his plan; he had
no plan beyond killing Amato. But as the desperate illogical
hope grew in him, he heard the launch's motors turn over
and kick throbbingly to life. "Wait!" he shouted, but the
crescendoing roar of the motors smothered his shrill, pleading voice.

When he reached the end of the terminal the small launch
was speeding out of the slip toward the river.

Neville braked his car to a skidding stop before Pier 17.

Another police squad was approaching on Ninth Street, its siren whining ominously in the darkness. "Watch yourself!" Neville yelled to Retnick, as he ran toward the pier with a gun in his hand.

Retnick was at his side when Neville kicked the door inward and stepped into the warehouse. A single light from the checker's office drew a bright circle on the thick heavy planking and here, in the middle of this brilliant pool, Nick Amato lay dying. Neville knelt beside him and pulled open his tie and collar. "Who did it, Nick?" he said.

"It was Joe. I could've saved him—" Amato's voice dropped away into a dry whisper.

"You're hurt badly," Neville said. "Help us now, Nick."

Retnick was staring down the length of the dark terminal. That's where Lye was. He glanced at Neville, and saw that he had put his gun on the floor while he worked on Amato's tie and collar.

"Is it like telling a priest?" Amato said, staring into Neville's eyes with terrible intensity.

"Who killed Glencannon?" Neville asked him quietly.

Retnick picked up the lieutenant's gun and walked into the terminal. In two strides he had merged with the darkness, and his big body became a shadow moving silently and deliberately toward the faint shifting lights on the river. The clouds had drifted in the high wind; the winter moon glinted on the water and coated the end of the wharf with a pale yellow glow.

Retnick couldn't think clearly; his thoughts circled hopelessly in a despairing maze. But he knew precisely what he was going to do. It was simple, inevitable choice. There was only one more thing for him to lose.

When he reached the wide doors that led to the open wharf he hesitated and stopped in the last few feet of darkness. Ahead of him was the bright arena; he could see the oil-soaked plankings, the stubby iron mooring posts, and a length of frayed rope that trailed down into the river. He glanced at his watch. 10:05. She was airborne now, settling comfortably in the deep reclining seat, leafing through a magazine or smoking a cigarette and watching the pinpoints of light on the ground.

The one who had brought him kindness and warmth and love was gone forever. Retnick was suddenly aware of a terrible knowledge; he was a stranger to himself, a stranger to this man who stood in the darkness waiting to die. This was a stalking animal who had reveled in the wrong done to him, putting that wrong above every other right. And Retnick saw him clearly now, studied him with eyes he had closed five years ago.

He hesitated no longer. With the gun hanging at his side he stepped onto the open wharf. The old wind struck his body, chilling the tears on his face and then above the noise of it, he heard Joe Lye shout: "Don't move, Retnick!"

Retnick turned toward the shrill voice. Lye stood against the wall of the warehouse on his left, his body thin and black in the pale light. The sight on the barrel of his gun gleamed like a splinter of ice.

"You can try shooting if you want," he cried.

"I'm through shooting," Retnick said in a weary, hopeless voice. "Somebody else will have to kill you, Joe. A dozen cops are on the way. Any of them will enjoy the job." The gun fell from his limp fingers.

From the darkness behind him a voice shouted his name and he heard the sound of running footsteps.

"Pick up that gun!" Lye screamed.

For a turbulent instant, Retnick regretted his decision; perhaps he could have paid the price if he lived. But it was too late to think of it.

"You get it in the stomach," Lye shouted at him. "Pick up your gun."

And Retnick knew then that Lye wanted to be killed, too. They were both looking for the easy way out. "You're wasting your time, Joe," he said. "You might as well toss your gun into the river."

"They won't take me back," Lye yelled, and put the gun to his temple. For an instant that seemed frozen in time he swayed back and forth, while his lips twisted into a helpless frenzied smile. And then he began to sob terribly; the gun dropped from his fingers and he went slowly down to his knees. The strength seemed to have been squeezed from his body. He fell over onto his side, and the sound of his weeping was like that of a lost and frightened child.

There were three uniformed patrolmen behind Lieutenant Neville when he came out of the terminal onto the wharf. He gave a short order, and two of them hauled Lye to his feet while a third picked up the gun that had fallen from his hand. Then he glanced at Retnick, who was staring at the river. "You okay?" he said, still breathing hard.

"Sure."

Neville looked at Lye and said, "You're going back to the death house, clever boy."

Lye's face was as blank as an idiot's. "I never left there," he said in a soft wondering voice, as if this were something Neville should realize.

Neville nodded at the cops who held his arms. "Get him out of here." When they had gone he looked at Retnick and then at his own gun which was lying on the thick planking of the wharf. Picking it up, he studied it with a little frown. "You didn't mean to use it, I guess," he said.

"That's right," Retnick said. "It seemed like a good idea at the time." He shrugged heavily, staring at the dancing lights on the water. "Like most good ideas it didn't work."

"We got an earful from Amato," Neville said, watching Retnick's face with a frown. "Glencannon, Dixie Davis, the works. Aren't you interested?"

"Sure, it's great," Retnick said heavily.

"And Joe Ventra. Amato killed him, Steve. That will be part of the newspaper story. You're in the clear. Isn't that what you wanted?"

"I was in the clear when I went to jail," Retnick said. "Now that I'm clear I'm guilty. That's a cute twist, isn't it?" The moment of dual perception was gone; there were no longer two men in his mind, there was only one. Retnick, who had taken what he wanted and couldn't pay the price. The moral bankrupt. That was the man he had to live with;

the man who could hold him in judgment had died five years ago.

"Steve, part of what you accomplished was good," Neville said, seeing the pain in Retnick's eyes.

"Part of it," Retnick said bitterly. "How's Kleyburg?"

"One of the boys in the squad heard a report. He's got a better than even chance. The old man lived a healthy life and that's working for him now."

Retnick looked at him. "They think he'll live?"

"It looks good," Neville said. "I said you couldn't help him a while ago. But I could be wrong. Will you go to see him tomorrow?"

This would be the start of it, Retnick knew. The payment. "Yes, I'll see him," he said slowly.

Neville glanced at his watch and said awkwardly, "Well, I've got work to do, Steve. We can talk about this later."

"Sure, let's go."

Neville caught his arm. In the moonlight Retnick saw the little smile on his lips. "I meant that. You know where I am. I'll expect to see you."

"Sure," Retnick said, in a different voice. The lieutenant's words reminded him of what Kleyburg had said: *Most people are decent. They want to help.* "I'll see you around, lieutenant."

It was almost eleven o'clock when Retnick let himself into the hallway of his rooming house. He had walked here from Pier 17, simply because he had nowhere else to go; even the thought of stopping for a drink had left him without enthusiasm. What was there to celebrate? And getting drunk wouldn't help. There were no easy outs. He had learned that much.

Mrs. Cara looked out of her room at him and said, "You got a phone call to make." She came down the hallway, holding her blue flannel robe tightly about her throat. In the soft overhead light her olive-dark eyes were bright with excitement. "It's important. It's from your wife."

"My wife?" Retnick said, and a little chill went through him. "You're sure?"

"That's what she said."

"Did she call from the airport?"

"No, she was home." Mrs. Cara watched him with frank curiosity. "You going to call her?"

Retnick couldn't answer her; his throat was suddenly tight. Turning he went quickly down the hall to the telephone. Marcia answered the first ring and said, "Yes? Hello?"

She'd been waiting at the phone, he thought, and a hope that was sharper than pain went through him. "This is Steve," he said. "You called me."

"I switched over to an early morning flight," she said. "You told me your job might be over and—I wanted to be sure you were all right."

"Everything is over," he said thickly. She'd switched flights, that was all. Hearing her voice now was almost more than he could bear.

"You don't sound too cheerful about it."

"It's—" His fist suddenly tightened on the receiver. "I need you, baby," he said, in a harsh and desperate voice. "I need you," he said again, feeling a tremor shake his body. "You don't owe me anything. It's the other way around. And I can't pay you back. Ever. But let me see you before you go."

She didn't answer him for a moment. Then she said unsteadily, "I thought we'd been over everything important, but—I could be wrong. Do you remember that bar on Seventieth? Tony's?"

"Yes, sure." He stood, breathing as if he had run a race. "I can be there in ten minutes."

"I'll be waiting for you," she said, in a voice so low that he barely heard the words. Then she hung up.

Retnick went down the hall to the doorway, and Mrs. Cara smiled at him and said, "You going out?"

"Yes, I've got to," he said, hardly conscious of her presence. But with a hand on the door, he turned to her. "You'd better look after the cat," he said.

"You're not coming back?"

"I don't know. I hope not." Then he became aware of

her smile. "I guess you understand," he said.

"I'll take care of Silvy," she said. "You go home."

Retnick opened the door and went quickly down to the street. In the pale moonlight a soft snow was falling gently over the city. Turning up his collar he started for the avenue where he knew he could find a cab. And then he began to run.